A Murder Solved Twice

Also By Murray Moffatt

A Different Kind of Life (Autobiography)

Play

**Murder Best Unsolved*

**Murder Maybe Relative*

**Murder Maybe By Evil*

Murder And No Play

**Murder Sometimes Cold*

**Murder Not Quite Buried*

**A Murder Solved Twice*

**A Shane Daniels Mystery*

A Murder Solved Twice
A Shane Daniels Mystery

A Novel by
Murray Moffatt

ISBN: 978-1-7782065-9-7

Cover Design: Murray Moffatt, Jill Moffatt, Sarah Autio

Author's Note:

I've always liked a good courtroom drama, either in a book, film or television series and have incorporated it in several of my novels, in particular 'Play' and 'Murder And No Play'.

My enjoyment of the mind games and verbal battles between defence and prosecution lawyers, and between lawyers and witnesses goes all the way back to when I was a kid and watched the original Perry Mason series on my parent's old black and white television.

And even though I was very young at the time, I realized it was unrealistic that in every episode, Perry beat DA Hamilton Burger and unveiled the real killer. I still watch the original Law and Order, and look forward to the second half of the show when the case goes to court.

Early in my broadcasting career, I did have the opportunity to cover a few trials as a reporter, but most of them took place in Provincial Court and I only remember reporting on one murder trial that was held in the Superior Court.

That was a long time ago and until I started doing research for this novel, I was probably like many of you and most of what I knew about criminal law and trials came from American TV and movies.

But a second-degree murder trial is a key element in 'A Murder Solved Twice' so I've tried to be as accurate as possible regarding Canadian criminal trial laws and procedures. Any mistakes are mine or invented for dramatic purposes.

I'm having a great time writing new entries into the Shane Daniels Mystery series and really appreciate the feedback I get about the main characters.

 In particular, the expansion of Emma's role in the stories and the colourful antics of Shane's friend, Ben Chen, who makes me smile every time I write about him.

Once again, I want to extend a sincere thank you to everyone who has taken the time to read my novels and for all of the support and encouragement of my retirement hobby.

As always, my love and appreciation for my wife Jill who does the thankless job of proofreading my work and to my daughters, Sarah and Laura, for their love and support.

This is a work of fiction. Names, characters and incidents are all products of my imagination. Any mistakes are mine alone.

Murray Moffatt
May 2024

For anyone who has read anything I've written because it means so much to me

"Trust your hunches. They're usually based on facts filed away just below the conscious level."
American Psychiatrist Dr. Joyce Brothers

"Probably the toughest time in anyone's life is when you have to murder a loved one because they're the devil."
Comedian Emo Philips

Chapter One - Present

When Shane Daniels opened his eyes he saw nothing but darkness and in a panic, thinking he had gone blind, he closed his eyelids and started rubbing them with his fists.

Then came the pain.

His eyes burned like he had been sprayed with mace, something he was familiar with because he had it done voluntarily when he was a rookie cop, just so he would know what it felt like. And he had a pounding headache, like the worst migraine he would suffer when he was under a lot of stress.

The burning eyes, the headache and the thought that he may have been blinded had Shane's heart thumping against his chest and sweat started rolling down his face.

Shane was on his back on what felt like a smooth concrete floor and some of the panic subsided as he realized he was in some type of sealed room where there was no light of any kind, so he was most likely not blind. He sat up and felt a wave of nausea join his pounding head, burning bile rose into his throat and he fought back the urge to vomit. What the hell! Shane thought as he tried to stand up, but then thought the better of it and returned to sitting on the hard floor. Other than weakness, it didn't feel like he had suffered any physical injuries and after running his hands over the golf shirt and jeans he was wearing he didn't find any tears or feel any dampness. He still had his running shoes on and the bottoms felt clean and dry.

The burning in Shane's eyes had subsided and both the nausea and headache felt like they were easing. What kind of drug was I injected with and why? Shane asked himself. Where am I? How long have I been here? Who did this and what do they want?

Shane thought about the last thing he remembered; getting into his car in the small parking lot at the back of Burke and Associates, the Brantford law firm he worked for. He used to try and find a parking spot on King Street, in front of the building, but his employer, Jason Burke, had finally made good on his promise to find a space for Shane's Dodge Charger in the employee parking lot. Shane being forced to park his classic muscle car on the street had been a standing joke between Shane and Jason, who was not only his boss but a good friend.

"I just assumed you would want your beloved vehicle to be on the street and visible so people driving by can admire it," Jason would tease.

"You assumed wrong," Shane would reply, putting indignation in his voice. "A 1969 Dodge Charger in mint condition sitting on a street in downtown Brantford, especially after hours, is a magnet for car thieves. I might as well put a 'Steal Me' sign on it."

"You can submit the cost of the sign with your monthly expenses if you wish," Jason deadpanned.

"That's big of you, Jason," Shane said. "How about just getting me a spot at the back like you promised."

But it was in that secluded parking area behind the law firm that Shane became the victim of not a car thief, but rather a kidnapper.

He remembered it was noon when he left the office through the back door on his way to get a sandwich and coffee for lunch. The Charger was the only vehicle in the lot because everyone else who parked there had either already left for lunch or perhaps for home since it was Friday and some employees only worked a half day heading into the weekend. Shane remembered pushing the button on his key fob to turn off the alarm system he had installed in the Charger, unlocking the door and getting into the driver's seat, and then a sharp pain in the back of his neck. That was all until he woke up lying on his back in this pitch-black room.

Shane decided not to try standing up until the dizziness he was feeling was gone, so he turned from his sitting position and got on his hands and knees. He searched with his hands in the area around him, but as he expected, the kidnapper hadn't left Shane's cane behind. He crawled slowly forward then stopped and waved one hand in front of him. After doing the same thing four or five times, Shane's outstretched hand touched a wall and after running his palm back and forth over the surface, he figured it was an unpainted wallboard.

Suddenly, a light came on and Shane squeezed his eyes shut against the brightness that felt like someone had turned on a high-intensity flashlight right in front of his face. It was as if black spots had been permanently burned into his irises, which would have been wide open in the dark to try and take in any available light. Shane opened his eyes and started blinking until they adjusted to the light, the black spots still there but starting to fade.

The illumination was coming from a round, flat fixture recessed into the ceiling and while it hurt like hell when it first came on, it was a low wattage bulb filling the room with a soft light. There was, as Shane suspected, a concrete floor and the room was probably twelve by twelve feet. All of the walls were covered by wallboard and so was the ceiling, but no plaster had been applied to cover the seams where the boards met or the indentations left by the screws. There was the outline of a door on the wall Shane was facing, but no outside hinges or a doorknob were visible. About three-quarters of the way up the door, there were hinges on the bottom of what looked like a rectangle-shaped trapdoor, but no inside handle.

On the floor, in the corner to the left of the door, Shane saw a plastic pail he assumed he was supposed to use as a toilet and a tray holding a small plate with a sandwich on it and a bottle of water. Shane wasn't hungry but his mouth was dry and his throat was sore, so he decided to go for the water. He tried standing up, did manage to get to his feet and take two small steps, but vertigo hit him hard and it took all of his concentration not to fall. Then, just as the dizziness and the room-spinning sensation started to ease, the intense nausea returned and Shane could feel the contents of his stomach making its way up into his throat. He dropped to his knees and crawled quickly, managing to make it in time to throw up into the pail. And after he had vomited everything that was in his stomach, he suffered severe dry heaves for at least thirty seconds.

Exhausted, his sides hurting from the prolonged physical effort to throw up, Shane sat down and grabbed the bottle of water. The cap was sealed, so the bottle hadn't already been opened. Shane swished some water around in his mouth to take away the bad taste of the vomit and spit it into the pail. He then drank down over half the bottle to slake the incredible thirst he had.

The vertigo was still there and the headache and nausea that Shane thought was easing off had now returned in full force. I'm having a severe reaction to whatever the kidnapper injected me with to knock me out, Shane realized, and he worried he was going to need emergency medical attention which was not likely forthcoming.

Shane laid back down on the concrete floor, curled into the fetal position, and blacked out.

Chapter Two - Present

Emma Carstairs was nearing the end of her run and she was pushing herself to improve her time for completing five kilometers.

Her t-shirt was soaked with sweat and even though the afternoon temperature was just above the freezing mark, she was wearing shorts for the run, which allowed her to use the prosthetic running blade on her amputated left leg. She had become very proficient at running with the blade leg; its curved shape and carbon fibre construction made it light and springy, allowing runners to achieve greater speed than with traditional prosthetics.

After arriving back at her house on a quiet street in west Brantford, Emma checked her watch and noted she had been unable to cut even a few seconds off her run time and thought perhaps she had hit her ceiling for that distance. Can't think like that, she admonished herself, just got to keep pushing. Emma was proud of the athletic figure she had managed to maintain and although long distance running was fairly new for her, she had been doing calisthenics, weights and wind sprints since she started doing track and field in elementary school.

Emma had a flawless light complexion, petite features and blue eyes, all indications of her Nordic heritage. She normally wore little makeup and kept her natural blonde hair cut very short. Shane, who didn't have a big enough ego to realize how good looking he was, frequently told her how lucky he was that such a beautiful woman would want to be with him.

Emma had just enough time to shower and change before she went down to the street in front of the house to meet Lan's bus. There was an elementary school in the neighbourhood for Lan to attend, but at the start of the school year, her teacher and the Principal told Emma they wanted to advance Lan three grades and suggested she attend an enrichment school in the city's north end.

"As you no doubt know, Lan is a very smart young girl, with advanced skills in most subjects, but particularly in math, arts and languages," Principal Jim Sterne had told Emma. "There's a good chance she could complete the elementary curriculum within the next two years. I know it will likely be an inconvenience for both Lan and you, but I believe she would really benefit from taking the bus each day to the enrichment centre."

Emma talked to Lan about it and the young girl, who had recently turned nine years old, was excited about the idea. Shane and Emma had to make adjustments to their work schedules so someone was always at home to make sure Lan got on and off the bus every day. Emma was surprised and pleased with how accommodating the management at Brantford General Hospital, where she worked as an operating room nurse, had been about adjusting her shift schedule. So far, it had worked out that Emma was at home most mornings and always there to meet Lan's bus in the afternoon.

Emma was still doing some volunteer counselling for her friend, Psychiatrist Charlene Anderson, but was only handling one client at a time. Emma lost her left leg from the knee down in a landmine explosion when she was an explosives disposal expert with the Canadian Forces and since returning to the private sector she has been helping other amputees adjust to life with a prosthetic.

It had been a year since Lan Pham had come to live with Emma and Shane, and they couldn't be happier having the precocious young girl in their lives, especially Emma, who fell in love with Lan the moment she first saw her in a surgical ward bed at the BGH. Lan's parents were killed when their vehicle was deliberately forced off Highway 403 and while Lan survived, her right hand was crushed in the collision and had to be amputated.

The accident was caused by two members of a Vietnamese-Canadian gang who were trying to recover a bag of cash Lan's parents had taken from the home where they lived. The house, owned by the gang, had a cannabis resin extraction lab in the basement and was also used as a collection location for the hundreds of thousands of dollars the criminal organization earned from its various home-based labs around southern Ontario.

Lan and her parents had come to Canada from Vietnam through a landed immigrant sponsorship organization which was legitimate on the surface but was in reality a scam run by the gang to extract money from families looking for a way to get into the country. To pay off what they owed, families like the Phams were forced to live in homes with extraction labs that were located in higher-end subdivisions, the idea being not to draw any suspicion to the house.

After her parents were killed, the gang tried twice to silence Lan so she couldn't testify about who or what she saw at her house. A man managed to get into her room when she was still in the hospital but was interrupted as he was issuing a warning to Lan and he managed to escape. The RCMP wanted to move Lan to a secure facility outside of Brantford until they were able to shut down the criminal organization here in Canada as well as find out if she had any relatives in Vietnam. Emma, who by that time was deeply attached to the young girl, refused to let the authorities take Lan out of the city, arguing that she had already been traumatized enough by the death of her parents and the amputation of her right hand. Emma managed to convince the police and authorities with Family and Children Services to let Lan live with her and Shane in their well-secured home, something Lan said she wanted to do.

During the second attempt to silence Lan, two armed men managed to bypass the alarm system at Emma's house thanks to the complicity of a FACS councillor who stole the code to the alarm during one of her visits. During a confrontation, Emma shot and killed one of the intruders and wounded the other.

Now, a year later, the trauma both Lan and Emma suffered as a result of those events had slowly faded away and they had settled into a normal domestic routine. There had been no word from the bureaucratic-heavy Vietnamese government about any success in finding out if Lan had any relatives. Emma and Shane were considered Lan's foster parents, but they had submitted all of the paperwork required so they could adopt the young girl and they were waiting, and hoping, for approval.

Lan's bus arrived and after she got off, Emma hugged her and they went into the house where Lan took off her coat, hung it in the front closet, put her heavy backpack in her bedroom and then went into the kitchen and sat at the table. Emma got Lan a juice box out of the fridge and some cookies from a container in the cupboard.

"So, how's it going at your new school?" Emma asked as she sat at the table next to Lan.

"I like it, I'm learning lots of new stuff," Lan answered as she munched on a cookie.

Lan was using her prosthetic hand to hold the juice box. After almost a year of practice, there were very few things Lan couldn't do with what she called her Star Wars bionic hand. The prosthetic used microprocessors to amplify the so-called myoelectric impulses that remained in Lan's arm after her hand was amputated and allowed her a near natural range of motion. The new hand prosthetic technology was a huge improvement over the traditional body-powered type which was operated by a combination of a body harness, upper-body muscles and the remaining limb, all connected with a cable.

The myoelectric hand was very expensive, but Emma and Shane were determined to make sure Lan had the best technology available. The government did fund a small portion of the cost, but Emma took out a thirty thousand dollar loan against the house to pay the rest. She was also aware the hand might not last more than five years because of the wear and tear and would have to be replaced, but she didn't care.

"Have you made any friends yet?" Emma asked as she and Lan sat at the kitchen table.

"Not really," Lan replied, then leaned close to Emma and whispered, "Some of them are weird and kinda nerdy."

Emma whispered back, "Well, sometimes super smart people can be weird and kinda nerdy."

"Does that include me?" Lan asked in a serious tone, but Emma could see Lan was trying not to smile.

"Maybe," Emma answered in a noncommittal tone.

Emma and Lan just looked at each other for a moment, both trying to keep a straight face, and then Lan giggled and said, "Yeah, maybe," which brought a huge smile to Emma's face and she leaned over and gave Lan a hug.

The teasing at the kitchen table was interrupted when the doorbell rang. Emma went to the entryway and activated the monitor on the security system panel to the left of the door which showed the view of the camera over the front step. Even though it had been a year since the attempt on Lan's life, Emma didn't let her guard down when it came to security.

After seeing on the monitor who it was, Emma opened the door and said, "Sergeant Singh! It's been a while. Come in."

"Hi Emma," RCMP Sgt. Gurdeep Singh said as he entered the house. Singh was dark-complected with fine facial features and along with his gray turban was wearing a dark blue suit, white shirt and a blue patterned tie. He was a sixteen year veteran of the Mounties and because of his knowledge of gang activities across Canada, served in joint organized crime task forces with various municipal police services.

Emma took Singh's overcoat and directed him to an easy chair in the living room, she sat on the sofa facing him and offered coffee, which he declined. A curious Lan entered the room and Singh said, "Hi, Lan!" and then asked, "How are you? Do you remember me?"

"You're the Mountie, Sergeant Singh, you arrested Maggie," Lan replied. Maggie Sawyer was Lan's Case Officer from Family and Children's Services, and after the attack in Emma's home a year ago, Singh arrested Maggie because she took a bribe from members of the Vietnamese-Canadian gang and supplied the security code to the house.

"Lan, do you want to go and watch some TV while I talk to Sergeant Singh?" Maggie asked.

"If you're going to talk about me, shouldn't I stay?" Lan asked in return.

Emma knew that Lan was smart enough to know Singh wouldn't be here unless it had something to do with the death of her parents and the people responsible. Emma also knew that because of the attempt on her life last year, Lan was well aware of the danger she could be in if something new came up in the case against members of the gang. Lan was a strong-willed and brave young girl, and Emma didn't want to upset her by suggesting she couldn't handle what Singh might have to say. However, Emma still felt she should get an idea of what was going on before including Lan.

"I have every intention of telling you if there's something new you should know," Emma told Lan. "But can I check it out first?" She asked.

Emma fully expected a push-back, but Lan said, "Okay, Emma, I can wait. Goodbye Sergeant Singh."

"Nice seeing you again, Lan," Singh said as Lan turned and left the room.

"So, Sergeant, what brings you there today?" Emma asked. "Not bad news, I hope."

"Four days ago, thanks to an alert Customs Officer, Hong Phuong was arrested at Vancouver Airport trying to get back into Canada with a false passport," Singh said. Phuong was the head of the Vietnamese-Canadian gang, based in Vaughn, north of Toronto, responsible for operating cannabis resin extraction labs in dozens of homes in cities and towns across Ontario. That included the one where Lan and her parents lived in Brantford. The gang also operated the bogus immigrant sponsorship program Lan's family got tangled up in and was reportedly involved in smuggling stolen goods into Canada.

A year ago, a joint task force involving the RCMP and members of several municipal police services had raided several homes with extraction labs, seizing hundreds of thousands of dollars in cash, equipment and weapons. Police did not make as many arrests as they had hoped and it was believed the gang was still operating.

Hong Phuong managed to elude arrest and flee the country, living in Vietnam until he attempted to get back into Canada. It was two of Hong's nephews that broke into Emma's house. She killed one and wounded the other, Quang Phuong, who was currently in jail awaiting trial.

"I'm most certainly glad to hear that Phuong is behind bars where he belongs, but that means there will be a trial and I assume you're here to tell me that Lan will have to testify," Emma said.

"I'm sorry Emma, I know it's something you wanted to avoid for Lan because of everything she's been through," Singh said. "But part of the case against Phuong will be establishing a direct link between him and the extraction labs. Lan saw Phuong visiting her parent's house on several occasions to check on the lab and we need Lan to testify to that. Once we have proven that link, we can not only get Phuong on the various drug and money laundering charges, we can also charge him with conspiracy to commit murder in the deaths of Lan's parents."

"Will her testimony have to be in person?" Emma asked. "Can it be on videotape or by camera from a different location?"

"The Canada Evidence Act has been amended several times in regards to testimony by children under the age of fourteen," Singh responded, "And there are allowances for young children to testify on videotape, by remote camera or behind a screen in the courtroom. But those are normally under exceptional circumstances, for example, a mental or physical handicap. There's no question that Lan will be judged capable of understanding the process and the courts have consistently ruled the defence in a trial has the right to question a child witness."

"So, how soon are we talking about?" Emma asked.

"Well, it'll likely be at least four months before a preliminary hearing is scheduled," Singh answered. "But the trial for Quang Phuong, the man you wounded, is coming up soon, although Lan was in her bedroom the entire time of the attack, so she likely won't have to testify. We've been trying to convince Quang to testify against his family in exchange for immunity, but he won't have any part of it.

His lawyer says Quang will plead guilty to break and enter but is not guilty of attempted murder. Quang claims he broke into your house looking for property to steal and you shot him for no reason."

"That's a good one," Emma said with a smile on her face.

Singh also smiled briefly, but then said in a serious tone, "Emma, with Hong Phuong back in Canada, in jail, and facing serious charges, I have to again express my concerns about Lan's safety, just as I did a year ago. Hong's gang is still operating and he's most likely still in charge, even though he was out of the country. That means he has people at his disposal to prevent Lan from testifying. She should be living at a secure, undisclosed location."

"No way!" Emma responded forcefully. "Lan is finally starting to live a normal life with a regular routine, making friends with kids her own age and attending a school for gifted children. The only reason those two guys got past our high-end home security system is because Maggie stole the code and that's not going to happen again. If I have to take another leave of absence from work to keep an even closer eye on her, then I will. But I can't allow her to be moved to another city, to live with strangers, and start all over again."

"Okay, Emma, I understand, but the Crown Prosecutor may feel differently," Singh said. "Quang didn't expect to be arrested entering the country. He figured he would sneak back into Canada and then disappear into the Vietnamese community in the Toronto area. He'll be desperate and that will put Lan in danger. You're only the foster mother and the Prosecutor might ask Family and Children's Services to take over Lan's care."

"I know, I'll have to prepare Lan for that possibility," Emma responded with sadness in her voice.

Emma and Singh discussed the situation for another ten minutes and after he left, Emma went to Lan's room and, as she had promised, explained to Lan what was going on. Lan, who had been sitting on her bed working on a drawing in the large sketchbook on her lap, remained silent while Emma spoke.

"I want to stay with you and Shane. I feel safe here," was all Lan said.

"I will try my best to make that happen," Emma responded.

A couple of hours later as she was just finishing preparing supper, Emma wondered why Shane wasn't home yet or hadn't called or texted he'd be late. She called his phone but got voicemail and then sent a text asking if he was going to be home for dinner. It's possible he got tied up doing surveillance and maybe had to turn his phone off, Emma thought. I'm sure he'll let me know what's going on.

Chapter Three - Present

When Shane woke up he had sweat running down his face but he felt chilled to the bone and his entire body was shivering.

The pounding headache and nausea were gone, which was good news, however he was light-headed and felt like he was stoned on something. He blinked rapidly to try and get his eyes to focus, but everything in the room where he was being held captive looked washed out and blurry.

Shane was sure he had taken a bad reaction to whatever drug his kidnapper had injected him with from the back seat of the Charger but wondered if whoever was holding him had come into the room while Shane was blacked out and injected him with something else.

He sat up and tried to clear his head, but the walls around him had taken on a red hue and the glare from the overhead light was hurting his eyes. He managed to focus on the tray that was still on the floor in front of him and wondered if the bottle of water he drank had been spiked with something. Shane remembered that the bottle was sealed but maybe a syringe with a very fine needle was inserted either through the cap or the soft plastic.

At this point, it doesn't really matter how it happened, Shane thought, I've been given a powerful drug of some kind and all I can do is try and ride it out. He then felt like there was someone else in the room and when he turned to the right, he saw his father sitting on the floor and leaning against the far wall.

"What was the name of the character Clint Eastwood played in his early TV western 'Rawhide'," his father asked.

"You always loved trying to stump me with trivia when I was a kid," Shane said, "But I don't have time for that now, I'm in trouble."

"Does that mean you don't know the answer?" his father asked.

"It's Rowdy Yates," Shane answered and then said, "You're not here, you're dead, you died over a year ago. And when you died, I was still angry with you and had a hard time trying to forgive you for all the lies you told me."

His father didn't respond and Shane saw that his dad looked thin and sickly, the way he looked when Shane saw him for the last time; sitting in a cell in Kingston Penitentiary waiting to die from terminal cancer. Ed Daniels had murdered his brother's young wife to complete a deal he made when his brother murdered Ed's wife, Shane's mother. Shane was seventeen years old at the time.

Shane closed his eyes and felt a wave of sadness, tears started running down his face. "Why did you ruin my life!" He cried out to his father. "You were supposed to be my dad, my friend, my hero, not a murderer!"

When he opened his eyes, Shane's father was gone, but Emma was there. "Oh no! They kidnapped you too!" Shane exclaimed, his sadness gone, replaced by panic. "Are you okay!? Did they hurt you!? Were you drugged!?"

Emma just smiled at him and said, "Come back, Shane", the famous line from the end of the movie he was named after. Shane tried to crawl over to where Emma was sitting, but his body felt like it was being forced to go in slow motion.

"I'm coming, Emma," he muttered as he struggled to move, his head down, trying to push against an invisible force. When he looked up, Emma was gone, replaced by a pretty young girl with long dark hair who looked to be around Lan's age.

"Who are you?" Shane asked. Was this another captive?

"I'm Rebecca, your sister," the young girl said with a smile.

Shane laid back down on the floor and covered his face with his hands. Whatever he was given, it was a very powerful hallucinogenic and he wasn't sure how much more he could take.

Rebecca was the name of his half-sister whose body was found beside her mother's remains just over a year ago in a wooded area just outside of his hometown of Paisley. Shane shot the man responsible for the murders, Ivan Barbarov, a former Russian GRU officer hiding out in Canada under the name Barber, and who had a young former prostitute from Moscow living with him. Barbarov had befriended Shane's father and up until just before Shane killed him, the Russian didn't know that Ed Daniels was the father of the child he thought was his. Even though he was dead, Shane still held a deep-seated hatred of Barbarov for killing a sister he would never know. Rebecca was two years old when she died, but somehow Shane's drug-addled brain had made her older.

"You are some fucked up, buddy," Shane heard his friend Ben Chen say. Shane took his hands away from his face and there was Ben, lying on the floor beside him, his face only about a foot away. "Looks like you were given a real special cocktail of fucking shit," Ben said. "The ass-wipe that did it really knows what he's doing when it came to hallucinogens."

Shane and Ben grew up together in Paisley, a village in southwestern Ontario, and despite being complete opposites, they had remained life-long friends and had been through a lot of adventures together. Ben, a Chinese-Canadian, something he never let anyone forget, ran a Chinese buffet restaurant in Port Elgin, a Lake Huron tourist town not far from Paisley.

Ben was short, slightly overweight, with fine Asian facial features. Shane was tall, well over six feet, a basketball star in college, very physically fit, with dark hair, and blue eyes. Shane had a quick temper, which he had worked very hard to overcome and was very measured when he spoke. Ben, on the other hand, had no filter and said whatever he felt like, often on purpose, because he enjoyed shocking people. During the entire time he had known him, Shane didn't think it was possible for Ben to go more than one sentence without a foul word in it.

"I don't know how much more of this I can take," Shane said to Ben.

"Maybe it's not drugs, maybe you're sick because you ate the fucking shit I serve at my restaurant," Ben said.

"Maybe. You're always telling me how bad it is," Shane replied. "You need to go away now, Ben."

Shane covered his face with his hands again and blacked out. When he regained consciousness, he was no longer lying on the floor but was sitting with his back against the wall facing the door. His watch had been removed when he was kidnapped so Shane had no idea how much time had passed since he found himself in this room or how long he had been unconscious. However, much to his relief, his head was clear from whatever drug he was given and the headache and nausea were gone.

Suddenly, the soft light in the room became so bright that when Shane closed his eyes against the glare he had the intense white spots on the back of his eyelids like you get if someone shines a flashlight close to your face. Then ear-splitting heavy metal rock music started and Shane jammed his pointer fingers into his ears against the blare, but it did little good. He had seen movies that showed how this kind of torture was used on prisoners for sleep deprivation and to break them down mentally for interrogation. But why him? What possible secret information did he have that they wanted? It made no sense.

Shane curled into the fetal position, pushing his eyes closed as hard as he could against the glare and keeping his fingers jammed into his ears. He tried to block out the screeching guitars and screaming vocals and concentrate on something else, but the music vibrated through his body and it felt like the bass guitar and drums were in his head rattling his brain.

Minutes seemed like hours as the light and sound assault continued and at one point Shane screamed in agony. He wasn't sure how long it went on, but the music finally stopped suddenly and the lighting in the room returned to normal. Shane took the fingers out of his ears and shook his head to try and clear it, but his ears were ringing with a high-pitched squeal. He opened his eyes and there were still black spots in front of them but, thankfully, they were fading quickly.

Shane sat up and leaned against the wall. He was incredibly thirsty and looked at the bottle of water sitting on the tray on the other side of the room. It's going to drive me crazy sitting there, he thought, but I can't drink it unless I want to go on another hallucinatory trip and see my father, Emma, Ben and a young woman who was supposed to be his dead half-sister.

Shane heard some noise coming from the other side of the hinge-less and knob-less door, like a latch being turned, and then watched as the rectangle trap door fell open downward on its hinges. A face appeared in the opening, a young man in his mid-twenties, Shane guessed, with a fair complexion, hair shaved close to his scalp and a neatly trimmed dark beard.

"Hello Shane Daniels," the young man said, "Do you remember me?"

Shane, whose ears were still ringing and felt like his brain was scrambled, looked at the young man and tried to figure out who he was. Then it came to him.

"You're Josh Benson, Gavin Benson's son," Shane stated and then asked, "Why am I here, Josh? Why are you drugging and torturing me?"

"Because you are responsible for my father's death," Josh replied.

Chapter Four - Before The Trial

"Okay, let's get started," Jason Burke said as he entered the conference room of his law firm, Burke and Associates, sat down in a plush, dark office chair at the head of the long oak table and set a manila file and note pad in front of him.

Already sitting at the table waiting for the meeting to begin were Shane, Chioma Abiola, the firm's Researcher, Jamie Wheeler, Jason's Law Clerk, and Elizabeth Pratt, one of the Legal Assistants. Everyone had a laptop on the conference table in front of them along with a pad of paper and pen. Jill Langly, the firm's long-time receptionist, who also served as Office Manager, had made sure there was a large thermos of coffee and a tray of muffins and donuts on the table for everyone to help themselves.

"I think it would be helpful if we go back to the beginning of the case and review what we know and don't know," Jason said.

Jason Burke was one of the most respected and successful criminal trial lawyers in Ontario. He was a big man, well over six feet and heavily built, which made him both an imposing and sometimes intimidating figure in the courtroom. Jason had a dark complexion, sharp features and silver hair combed straight back from his forehead. He and Shane's relationship had long ago gone beyond boss and employee, and they were now close friends and confidants.

"I'll start," Jason began. He pushed a key on his laptop and the screens on the other laptops started showing a series of crime scene and autopsy photos. "The partially clothed body of twenty two year old Paige Madison was discovered in a field off Powerline Road in the north end of the city by the owner of the property who was walking his dog at the time. Tire tracks indicate that a four-wheel drive vehicle was likely used to drive onto the field from the street in order to dump the body. An autopsy showed that Paige had been strangled, raped and sodomized. It also showed she was three months pregnant."

"Paige grew up in Brantford," Jason continued. "She was the only child of Bill and Anna Madison. She attended Brantford Collegiate here in the city and Conestoga College in Kitchener. At the time of her death, she was working as an Administrative Assistant at Grand River Associates, an engineering firm owned by Gavin Benson and Ethan Holdaway. Gavin Benson is our client. He's charged with second degree murder."

Jason looked over at Shane and said, "Shane, do you want to summarize the police investigation and why Gavin was charged?"

Shane opened a file on his laptop where he kept his notes and said, "The Pathologist, Heidi Vandersand, estimates that Paige was killed within approximately five hours prior to when her body was found and strangulation was the cause of death. Doctor Vandersand says the sexual assault on Paige was quite brutal and semen recovered from her body helped her determine the assault occurred within that five hour window."

"Detectives interviewed everyone associated with Paige, both personal and professional," Shane continued. "During his interview, a distraught Gavin Benson admitted that he and Paige had been having an affair. He said he was with Paige on the day she was murdered and said he did not know that she was pregnant. Detectives asked Gavin to voluntarily provide his DNA, which he did, and it was a match to the semen found in Paige's body and to her unborn child."

"Was Mr. Benson advised of his rights during that interview or when he agreed to provide a sample for DNA testing?" Jamie Wheeler asked.

"No, because at that point he was not being detained or arrested," Jason answered. "However, it's something we will be arguing in voir dire."

Under Canadian law, voir dire is a separate hearing during which a Judge rules whether evidence is admissible during the trial.

"If we can show that the Detectives already considered Gavin their main suspect before they interviewed him and requested his DNA and that they intended to arrest him no matter the outcome of the interview, then we can argue Gavin should have been told his right to legal representation," Jason continued. "If that's the case, we will argue the results of the DNA testing and anything Gavin told police during the interview is not admissible during the trial."

Shane then continued his narrative, telling the meeting that Benson was arrested and charged with second degree murder after police had completed their interviews with other people connected to the case and the DNA test results came back.

"Shane, can you give us an overview of the other players in the case?" Jason asked.

"No problem," Shane responded and then explained that Gavin Benson and his wife Alison have been married for twenty nine years, but since his arrest, she has filed for divorce. Alison says she had no idea her husband was having an affair with a woman around the same age as their children.

"The Bensons have two kids," Shane said, "A twenty four year old married daughter, Melissa Edwards and a twenty eight year old son, Josh, a Sergeant in the Canadian Forces, currently stationed at Camp Borden, north of Toronto. Melissa is currently on maternity leave with her first child. Her husband, Jake, works at a plumbing company here in the city. As mentioned, Benson is a partner in an engineering firm. The partner, Ethan Holdaway, is married and he and Benson are the same age, fifty two. The two men met at university and they've been in business together for over twenty years."

"Thanks, Shane," Jason said. "Now, as we all know, Gavin has pleaded not guilty and he insists he did not kill Paige. The Crown Prosecutor, in an attempt to avoid a trial, has offered a ten year prison sentence with no chance of parole if Gavin agrees to plead guilty to manslaughter. Gavin has turned that down. I have advised him that if he's found guilty at trial, the sentence is twenty five years with the earliest eligibility for parole at ten years, but that would be up to the Judge."

"Jason, I know you're the best chance he's got, but Benson must realize the case against him is, I'm sorry to say, looking open and shut," remarked Chioma, who normally didn't speak up at pretrial meetings. Chioma was a tall, beautiful black woman with short, very curly hair and multiple, small gold hoops along the outside of each ear. She immigrated to Canada from Nigeria with her husband and two young children and worked as a Researcher at Burke and Associates while she studied at night to get her law degree. Both of her children were now in university and she was in the late stages of her studies. Shane was happy Chioma was getting closer to her goal of becoming a lawyer, but she was an outstanding researcher and he was going to hate losing her from that position.

"Chioma, you don't have to apologize for voicing your opinion at a trial strategy meeting," Jason said. "We each need to be open and frank about how we see both the prosecution's and defence's positions. Gavin is aware that we face a significant challenge in trying to convince at least one member of the jury that he's not guilty."

Jason then gave an overview of the Crown's case against Benson. Gavin was the last person to see Paige alive on the day she was murdered. He says it was Paige's day off and he went to her apartment that morning, they had sex, and then he left for his office. In a statement to police, which Jason reviewed before Benton signed it, Gavin said that he and Paige were deeply in love, despite their age difference, and wanted to spend the rest of their lives together. Gavin stated that, as far as he knew, his wife was not aware of the affair, but he was planning to tell her that weekend and ask for a divorce. Gavin insisted he didn't know that Paige was pregnant and if she had told him, he would have been happy. He told the police that his partner, Ethan Holdaway, found out about the affair and had expressed serious concerns about it. In his statement, Gavin said he would never hurt Paige and he was devastated by her death.

"The receptionist at Grand River Associates will testify that Gavin was two hours late arriving at the office on the day of the murder, so the Prosecutor will argue his whereabouts are unaccounted for and he had time to kill Paige and dump her body in the field," Jason said. "As well, Gavin owns a four wheel drive Jeep Cherokee and a forensic specialist is prepared to testify that casts of the tire tracks in the field where the body was found show treads that match the type of tire on Benson's Jeep."

"The field was very muddy that day and those tread marks were not distinct," Shane commented, "I saw the casings and, at best, the forensic specialist can claim some general characteristics with the Goodyear tires on the Jeep."

"Tire treads and footprints are notoriously unreliable evidence and have been challenged many times in court," Jason responded. "I believe I can have the tire treads ruled inadmissible for the trial."

"Most certainly I can find out how many Jeep Cherokees with standard Goodyear tires are registered in the Brantford area and given how popular it is, there will be lots," Shane said and then added, "Forensic officers went over Benson's Jeep with a fine tooth comb and found no evidence that Paige was ever in the vehicle, so under Locard's Principle, you can argue that her body was not transported in the Jeep."

Under Locard's Principle, named after forensic science pioneer Doctor Edmond Locard, when there is contact between two items, there's always an exchange of material, often microscopic. If Paige's body was in the Jeep, some evidence would have been left behind.

"At this point, besides the forensic evidence, the biggest obstacle we face at trial is the testimonies of Ethan Holdaway, Gavin's partner, and Ariel Durst, Paige's best friend, because the Prosecutor will say they prove motive," Jason said. "Ariel's testimony will be particularly damaging and it will come down to the jury trying to decide between her credibility versus Gavin's."

Ariel and Paige had been close friends since childhood and according to Ariel, they never kept secrets from each other. Ariel says Paige told her in strictest confidence that she was having an affair with an older, married man, and that they were in love with each other. Paige eventually told Ariel her lover was Gavin Benson, one of her bosses, and she showed her friend his photograph on her phone. Ariel says she got angry at Paige for getting involved with a man old enough to be her father and urged her to break off the relationship, but she refused and admitted she was pregnant.

"Ariel will testify that Paige told her Gavin kept putting off asking his wife for a divorce and she had run out of patience," Jason said. "Ariel says the day before she was murdered, Paige told her she was going to tell Gavin that she was pregnant and that if he didn't ask his wife for a divorce, she was going to contact her and tell her what was going on"

"Ariel's testimony will most certainly show the jury Gavin had plenty of motive to kill Paige," Shane commented and then asked, "What about Holdaway?"

Jason answered by saying that Holdaway told police that he had suspected for some time that Gavin had something going on with Paige because of the way they acted around each other in the office. Holdaway confronted Benson about it and Gavin admitted he and Paige were involved. Holdaway says he demanded Gavin end the affair immediately and admonished him for possibly putting the company in serious legal and financial jeopardy because if the relationship ended badly, Paige could sue, claiming sexual harassment and intimidation by her employer to force her into having sex with him.

"Holdaway is prepared to testify that he and Gavin's partnership was already on shaky ground and he threatened to dissolve it if Gavin didn't end his relationship with Paige or if the affair became public," Jason told the meeting.

Jason looked at the faces of his colleagues and he knew that while no one was saying it out loud, they were all thinking that the Crown's case against Gavin Benson was solid and a successful defence was likely insurmountable.

"So, the question is, knowing what we do about the Crown's case, what possible defence do we have," Jason said. "The Judge will instruct the jury that in order to convict Gavin, the Crown must prove his guilt beyond a reasonable doubt. Outside of the semen, which would be expected since they were lovers, there is no physical evidence linking Gavin to Paige's murder. That leaves motive and opportunity. The Pathologist can't state an exact time of death because the body was left out in the elements, just a time frame before the discovery of the body. The receptionist says Gavin was late getting to work that day and we counter by saying, of course, he was late because he was having sex with Paige at her place. He was two hours late, but according to the Pathologist, there was another three hours after Gavin arrived at the office when Paige could have been killed and her body dumped in the field."

Jason saw Shane and Chioma nod their heads in agreement with what he said and then he continued. "Our strategy will be to raise as much reasonable doubt as possible about Gavin having a motive to kill Paige. Her friend, Ariel, says Paige was going to tell Gavin that she was pregnant and threaten to tell his wife if Gavin didn't ask her for a divorce, but what proof is there that Paige went through with it? As well, and this could be key to our strategy, if we keep looking into the motives and alibis of the other players in the case, perhaps we can present an alternative theory of who committed the murder."

Under Canadian law, an alternate suspect defence is allowed to raise reasonable doubt about the Crown's case. The alternate suspect can be someone directly involved in the case or a third party who hasn't been connected to the case by the police. The defence can present both direct and circumstantial evidence but it has to prove the alternate suspect has a direct connection to the case beyond just speculation and have an 'air of reality' before it can be presented.

"Shane, Chioma, I need you to keep working together to find out everything you can about the other people involved in the case," Jason said and then added, "Everyone's got a secret and we need to know if it has anything to do with our victim."

Jason closed his laptop, a signal that the meeting was concluded, so everyone else followed suit and started gathering up their notes and files.

"Jason," his law clerk, Jamie Wheeler, said as he stood up. "I know you're going to say it doesn't matter what we think, our job is to defend our client, but you're pretty famous around here for your gut feelings about a case. Can I ask what your gut is telling you about Benson's guilt or innocence?"

"I don't mean this as a smart ass remark, but right now all my gut is telling me is that it's time for lunch," Jason replied.

Chapter Five - Present

Emma's heart started beating faster and she felt a panic attack coming on when she woke up and saw that Shane's half of the bed had not been slept in.

Where the hell is he? she asked herself as she quickly slid out of bed, picked up her prosthetic leg and attached it to the stump on her left leg. After putting on her robe, which was lying on the foot of the bed, and some slippers, Emma headed for the kitchen.

Maybe he came in really late and I didn't hear him, Emma thought. She was normally a light sleeper but it was a long and stressful day yesterday after her discussion with Sgt. Singh about Lan testifying at a trial and she was tired. Maybe Shane slept on the couch so he wouldn't wake me up. Maybe he's in the kitchen. But Emma didn't smell any coffee, which she would expect if Shane was there, and when she walked in, all she saw was Lan sitting at the table eating a bowl of cereal and watching a video on her tablet.

"Morning, Emma," Lan said through a mouthful of Cheerios. "Where's Shane? He's always up first."

"He must have had to stay super late at his job," Emma replied. She felt there was no reason to share her worry about Shane's whereabouts with Lan and get her upset, which she would be because she and Shane had gotten close.

"You go ahead and finish your breakfast and get ready for school while I make a few calls to see what Shane's been up to," Emma said to Lan.

"Okay, Emma. Say hi to Shane for me when you talk to him," Lan said.

Emma walked out of the kitchen and down the hall to her bedroom while dialing Shane's number and like her numerous previous attempts, she got his voicemail. She left another message and then sent a text, again hoping that maybe Shane was in a situation where he couldn't answer his phone. Emma tried to push aside her fear that something bad had happened to Shane, hoping there was a reasonable explanation for his absence. Was it possible he was in an accident with that stupid classic muscle car of his? Shane loved his 1969 Charger, a gift from his father when he was sixteen, with its big V8 engine, sleek design, fat tires and leather interior. While Emma admired the car, she thought it was a deathtrap with its ability to travel at very high speeds and no safety features, like airbags. She was constantly trying to convince Shane to park it permanently in the garage and just admire it.

Emma knew she was going to have to contact the Brantford Police Service and the OPP to ask about accidents in the area, but she had a couple of other calls she wanted to try first. She knew that Office Manager Jill Langley always arrived early at Burke and Associates, so she called the private office line in order to bypass the switchboard and Jill answered right away.

"Jill, I'm trying to track down Shane. He didn't come home last night and I'm really worried," Emma said.

"Oh no," Jill responded with concern in her voice. "Shane went out at noon yesterday and told me he was going to pick up something to eat, but he didn't come back, and I just assumed he got a call and had to go somewhere for the rest of the day."

"Do you know what he was currently working on?" Emma asked, trying to keep the panic out of her voice, but probably wasn't doing a very good job of it. "Was it something that involved surveillance?"

"I'm not aware of anything and I normally have a pretty good idea of what people are doing," Jill answered and Emma knew that was true. Jill was the longest serving employee of Burke and Associates, starting on the day Jason first opened his practice, and was considered a bit of mother hen to the current staff, always anticipating their needs and patiently listening to their complaints.

"It's possible Shane was doing something directly for Jason that I don't know about," Jill suggested. "But Jason's not in yet for me to ask. Do you want me to call him at home?"

"No, I'll do that," Emma said and then added, "Thanks, Jill. If you hear from Shane, get him to call me right away."

"I will and don't worry, Emma, I'm sure there's a good reason why Shane hasn't been in contact," Jill said and while Emma appreciated her trying to sound positive about the situation, she knew Jill would also be very concerned.

After ending the call with Jill, Emma immediately dialed Jason Burke's cellphone first and if that didn't work, she'd call his landline at home. But Jason answered his cell after only two rings and after seeing her name on his call display, he said, "Hi Emma, how are you? What has you calling so bright and early in the morning?"

"Shane didn't come last night, I can't get in touch with him, he's missing and I'm worried sick. Is he on a special assignment for you?" Emma couldn't help herself because she was so worried, but she said all of this to Jason in one, quick, panic stricken sentence.

"Whoa, slow down! Shane's missing!?" Jason responded.

Emma took a deep breath to try and calm herself and repeated what she had said and asked, but a lot slower.

"No, I don't have him doing anything for me right now," Jason said. "As far as I know, Shane has been busy catching up on work for other lawyers that got delayed because of the Benson trial. I wasn't in the office much yesterday, so I didn't talk to him. Did you talk to Jill?"

"I did, just before I called you," Emma answered. "She said Shane left at noon yesterday and didn't come back, and has not been in touch."

"Okay, something has happened. Have you called the police yet? Maybe he was in an accident and couldn't call," Jason said, trying to sound calm and in charge.

"My next call," Emma responded. "I wanted to check and see if he was on something work related first, but I know he would have called me if that was the case."

"Call the police and they'll start a missing persons investigation immediately," Jason said. Unlike some American jurisdictions where a person is not considered officially missing until after twenty four hours, there is no waiting period in Canada.

"Emma, I don't want to upset you, but I have to ask," Jason said. "Is it possible Shane's disappearance has something to do with Lan's situation?"

"I don't know, I hope not," Emma answered. She explained the possibility that Lan could be in danger again because she'll have to testify against the leader of the Vietnamese-Canadian criminal organization who was recently arrested trying to get back into the country.

"We can't rule out the possibility that Shane has been taken to use as leverage against Lan," Jason stated.

"I've been too worried to think about stuff like that yet," Emma said.

"Okay, I'll hang up so you can contact the police. If you need anything, anything at all, you let me know," Jason said. "Once I'm showered and dressed, I'll be right over to your place to help out."

"Thanks, Jason," Emma said, disconnected the call and went to check on Lan, but the young girl was standing at the front door with her jacket on and wearing her backpack, ready to go and catch her bus.

Emma wondered if Lan had overheard her telephone conversations and her fear was confirmed when Lan asked, "Has something bad happened to Shane, Emma?"

Emma knew there was no point lying because Lan was smart enough to see right through it. "I don't know, but I hope not," Emma said. "I can't get in touch with him, but maybe there's a problem with his phone."

"It's more than that, isn't it?" Lan asked. "He didn't come home last night, did he?"

"No, but there could be a logical explanation for that," Emma answered, trying to sound as calm as possible, although she sure didn't feel that way. "Lan, I don't want you to worry about this, I'm sure it'll turn out that everything's fine with Shane. Let's get you on your bus."

Lan didn't say anything, but Emma could tell by the look on the young girl's face that she wasn't buying what Emma was telling her.

After watching Lan take her seat on the bus and waving to her as it pulled away, Emma realized that she had stood on the sidewalk in front of her house waiting with Lan while still in her robe and slippers. That's just great, she thought, the neighbours will think I'm too lazy to get dressed in the morning. I've got to get my head straight, she admonished herself, calm down, and get to work finding Shane.

Emma showered and dressed, found a photograph of Shane to take with her, and was on her way out the door to go to the police station to report him missing when she decided to try one more phone call, just in case.

She dialed Ben Chen's number, hoping he was awake. Although Ben's restaurant was in Port Elgin, he lived in Paisley in the house his parents left him when they passed away.

"Ben's Chinese gambling den! Our dice is honest, most of the fucking time," Ben answered.

"Don't you ever answer your phone by simply saying 'hi'?" Emma asked. While Shane thought his best friend was hilarious, Emma didn't understand Ben's warped sense of humour.

"Okay, hi Emma," Ben responded. "What's up with the early morning call?"

"Is there any chance you've talked to Shane over the past twenty four hours?" Emma asked.

"No, why? What's up?" Ben asked.

Emma was reluctant to say, but she knew she couldn't leave Ben hanging without an explanation for her call and question. She told Ben what was going on and that she was on her way to the police station to report Shane missing.

"I'm on my way!" Ben exclaimed.

"No, Ben, wait!" Emma said, but it was too late, Ben had hung up.

Christ! That's just what I need, Emma thought, Ben in Brantford, running around and getting in the way. I can't worry about that now, she concluded, I need to get to the police station.

Where are you, Shane?

Chapter Six - Present

Shane looked at Josh Benson's face staring at him from the opening in the door of the room where he was being held and asked, "What are you talking about Josh? Has something happened to your father?"

"You don't know? You haven't been told? My father hung himself in his cell at Millhaven two days ago. Another example of just how much you and your lawyer boss care about what happened to him," Josh answered with contempt.

"I didn't know, I hadn't been told yet," Shane responded. "I'm so sorry to hear that."

"Save your condolences. He wouldn't have even been in prison if you and Jason Burke had done more to prove his innocence!" Josh said angrily.

"So, in revenge for your father's suicide, you've kidnapped me, given me some kind of hallucinogenic drug and tortured me with loud music and bright lights," Shane responded. "As I said, I'm sorry about your dad, but what you're doing to me is not going to bring him back and, instead, you'll be going to jail and ruining your military career."

Shane got up slowly from where he was sitting against the back wall, still feeling a bit shaky, took several steps toward the door, and said, "Open the door and let me out, Josh, and we can talk this through.

You've reacted out of grief and anger, and I can talk to the police, tell them that this was an unfortunate mistake and see if I can convince them not to charge you."

"You don't get it, do you?" Josh said. "I don't care what happens to me and you're not going anywhere until you solve Paige's murder and clear my father's name. He's not going to die in prison and be forever remembered as a killer."

"Josh, you were in the courtroom for the trial, so you know that Jason did everything he could to prove your father's innocence or at least raise reasonable doubt," Shane said. "But the jury decided he was guilty. Jason felt there were definite grounds for an appeal and your father knew that."

"He knew it was likely going to take a couple of years to get an appeal into the court and he would be sitting in a cell, an innocent man, waiting for that to happen," Josh said. "He also knew the odds of him winning a new trial were slim and he was facing life in prison with no chance of parole for twenty five years. He couldn't do it."

"Josh, I worked very hard on your father's case," Shane said. "I investigated everyone, including people who were, at best, remotely involved. I checked and double-checked alibis, and I tried everything I could to find an alternative suspect or theory about the murder that Jason could use during the trial. I'm sorry Josh, but have you at least considered the fact that your father was guilty and he was lying when he said he didn't murder Paige?"

"Is that what you and Burke tell yourselves so you have a clear conscience about not doing enough to defend an innocent man?" Josh asked angrily and then added, emphasizing every word one at a time, "My. Father. Did. Not. Kill. Paige!"

Josh's light complexion had gone a deep red during this angry outburst and it was followed by silence as he and Shane stared at each other. Shane, who was feeling weak and exhausted from the drug and the lack of sleep, food and water, rubbed his face with his hands and said calmly, "Okay, Josh, let's agree your father was innocent, and both Jason and I have never said we didn't believe him, but there's not much I can do while you have me locked in this room, pumped full of drugs and being tortured by bright lights and ear-splitting music."

Josh didn't say anything and his face disappeared momentarily from the hole in the door. When he returned, he reached through the opening with a thick file held together with elastic bands and dropped it on the floor where the thump it made echoed through the room.

"That is a copy of the entire trial transcript," He said.

"And, what? You expect me to read through that and find something that proves your father's innocence or tells me who the real killer is?" Shane asked. "I'm more than familiar with what happened at the trial, Josh, and I don't think there's anything in the transcript that's going to make me go 'Aha!' like some TV Detective."

"It's a start, I'll get you some more resources," Josh said.

"How about you let me out of here and I promise I will vigorously re-investigate your father's case," Shane pleaded.

"Not happening. You better get reading," Josh said and his face disappeared from the opening in the door.

"Wait! Wait!" Shane called out and lunged toward the opening.

Josh's face reappeared and he yelled, "Back away from the door or I'll fill the room with a gas that will have you hallucinating for days!"

Shane did as he was told and after momentarily disappearing again, Josh returned and held a tray through the opening containing a plate of spaghetti, a small bread roll, an orange, a plastic fork and two bottles of water.

"Take this. I promise you none of it contains drugs. What I've done to you up until this point was to demonstrate what happens if you don't do what you're told. But I want your head clear from now on," Josh said.

Shane walked over, took the tray, and backed up from the door.

"Josh, listen to me," he said, but Josh reached in and pulled the trap door closed and Shane heard the click as it was locked.

This has got to be some kind of bizarre nightmare, Shane thought, as he set the tray on the floor and then sat down.

He opened one of the bottles of water and took a long drink, hoping Josh was telling the truth when he said it wasn't spiked. Resigned to his situation, Shane set the water bottle down, picked up the trial transcript, and started reading.

Chapter Seven - The Trial

"Doctor Vandersand, were you able to determine if the sexual assault on Paige Madison occurred before or after she was strangled?" Crown Prosecutor Evan Gregory asked.

Pathologist Heidi Vandersand had already been on the witness stand at the Gavin Benson murder trial for half an hour, but most of that time had been taken up establishing her credentials and reviewing the autopsy results regarding time and cause of death.

Vandersand was in her mid-fifties, a tall, thin woman with short silver-blonde hair and a pale complexion. She wore no makeup or jewelry and was dressed for court in a dark blue pantsuit and a pale white blouse, sitting with a very erect posture and giving everyone in the courtroom, in particular the jury, the impression of someone highly competent and all business.

"The assault took place before death," she answered Gregory's question.

"And you were able to determine that she was restrained while this occurred," Gregory said.

"Yes. There were ligature marks on Ms. Madison's wrists and ankles, and when we examined the discolourization on her skin from the bruising and compared them to other results, such as the timing of lividity, we determined she was tied up, likely with plastic rope, and still alive, when she was assaulted," Vandersand replied.

The Prosecutor paused, on purpose, to let the jury think about what Vandersand said and to consider how Paige Madison must have suffered before she was killed.

Evan Gregory was a short, rotund man, dark-complected with a nose that looked like it had been broken a few times, and thinning hair. Both he and Jason Burke, who was sitting with Gavin Benson at the defence table, were dressed in the traditional clothing worn by lawyers appearing in the Superior Court of Justice; gray striped dress pants, white collared shirt, waistcoat, a long black robe and white tabs, which looked like wings hanging down the front of the robe.

"Doctor Vandersand, your report says Ms. Madison was violated vaginally and anally, is that correct?" Gregory asked.

"Yes, she was penetrated with a foreign object," Vandersand answered.

"Do you know, or can you offer a professional opinion, based on your experience, what kind of object was used?" Gregory asked.

"I can't say for certain, but the damage to the victim's vagina and rectum suggests the item was three to five inches around, about the size of a wooden broom handle," Vandersand responded.

The Pathologist's answer caused a stir and murmuring of voices from the people sitting in the courtroom, many of them family and friends of Paige's. Gregory was content to stand in front of his table and look gravelly at the jury, several of whom appeared upset about what they had heard and many looked over at Gavin who had no expression on his face and was looking down at the table in front of him.

The situation was not lost on Jason, who knew this testimony was coming and was well aware of the impact it would have on the jury. He kept a neutral expression on his face because he knew the jury would be looking at him and Gavin, but he had told Gavin it was okay to be emotional during this testimony because it was about what happened to the woman he loved. However, he noticed out of the corner of his eye that his client had reacted stoically.

"Doctor Vandersand," Gregory continued after his pause for effect, "Based on your examination, would it be safe to say the brutal sexual assault on Paige was done out of anger and hate?"

"Your Honour," Jason said as he stood up, "Doctor Vandersand is an expert Pathologist, but I respectfully submit cannot testify to the motivation and emotional state of the perpetrator of the assault."

"I would tend to agree," Judge Garnet said. Garnet was a veteran Superior Court Judge, serving for more than twenty five years and was well respected by both prosecution and defence attorneys. Around the courthouse, people would often remark that Garnet had a striking resemblance to actor Tommy Lee Jones.

"I believe the facts presented by Doctor Vandersand will speak for themselves," Garnet said, "But any opinions or speculation regarding what they mean in terms of the perpetrator's state of mind should be left to experts in criminal psychology. Mr. Gregory, do you have any other questions for Doctor Vandersand."

"No, your Honour, I'm finished with the witness," the Prosecutor answered.

"Mr. Burke, you may proceed," Garnet said, looking over the reading glasses he always had perched on the end of his nose when the court was in session.

"Your Honour, Doctor Vandersand was quite thorough in her testimony, so I have no questions," Jason said.

"Very well," the Judge said. "In that case, I think we will adjourn now for the lunch break and resume at one pm." Garnet then stood up and everyone in the courtroom did the same until the Judge left through a side door.

Jason turned to Gavin and said, "They'll be bringing you lunch in the holding area and I thought we could talk while you're eating. I'm going to bring Shane with me if that's okay."

"Fine," Gavin said as the court security officer came and led him away and Jason noted his client appeared upset.

Ten minutes later, Jason, Shane and Gavin were sitting together at a metal table in a small interview room off the area where the holding cells for prisoners waiting to appear in one of the various courtrooms were located. Gavin had been brought a tray holding a sandwich, soup in a small styrofoam container, a pint of milk, coffee in a paper cup and an orange. When Jason and Shane arrived, Gavin hadn't touched any of the items on the tray and when they sat down he said, "The people on the jury were looking at me like I was some kind of sick, twisted monster. They're not going to forget what the Pathologist said I did to Paige."

"In a murder trial, the results of the post-mortem on the victim are always difficult to hear," Jason said.

"Their faces told me I'm as good as guilty," Gavin lamented.

"Gavin, listen to me, the trial is in its early stages," Jason said. "The Crown is laying out its case and if the Prosecutor does his job, everything will look bad for you so, of course, you're going to get a lot of looks from members of the jury. My job is to counter by punching holes in the Crown's case and show that there's a lot of reasonable doubt that you're guilty. We're just getting started."

"I know I don't show my emotions, but it's eating me up inside when they talk about what happened to Paige in such a clinical way," Gavin said. "She was so beautiful and smart, she made me feel alive for the first time in longer than I care to remember."

Even as he said this, Jason could see that Gavin was right when he said he wasn't an overtly emotional person. His client's face gave no indication of what he said he was feeling.

Benton was a handsome man who looked a lot younger than his age; a trim, athletic body from working out at a gym three times a week, piercing green eyes and sharp features, short dark hair parted to the side with just a touch of gray at the temples. Jason could see why a young woman like Paige would be attracted to Gavin and that their age difference wouldn't matter.

Shane spoke up for the first time. "Gavin, I've been going back over the alibis for the time of the murder of everyone connected to the case, but I'm not finding any holes," he said and then asked, "Are you sure there's no one else I haven't talk to who would have a grudge against you or Paige, someone Paige mentioned she was having trouble with, someone who knew about the affair and would be angry about it? Maybe an old boyfriend?"

"As far as I know, no one knew about our affair until my partner, Ethan, confronted me about it," Gavin replied. "I didn't know Paige had told her friend, Ariel, until I heard she was going to testify. Paige told me she never had a steady boyfriend and hadn't been seeing anyone for a couple of years before we got together."

"I know I've asked you this several times already leading up to the trial, but now that you've had more time to think about it, are you absolutely sure your wife didn't know or suspect you were having an affair? Or maybe your daughter, Melissa?" Shane asked.

Gavin responded by reiterating what he had told Shane and Jason previously, that he and his wife, Alison, had been living basically separate lives since their kids left home and they became empty nesters. He immersed himself in work and she substantially increased her already busy community service, including Chairing the United Way Board and preparing a campaign to run for the

School Board in the fall municipal election. Gavin said that he and his daughter, Melissa, were never particularly close and he hadn't see her very much in recent years, especially after she got married to Jake, who Gavin didn't like and the feeling was mutual.

Jason and Shane left Gavin in the holding area and went to get their own lunch at one of the restaurants near the Wellington Street courthouse. The sky was overcast but it was a warm day and Shane removed his suit jacket to carry over his arm, while Jason had already left his long dark robe in a room at the courthouse set aside for solicitors.

As they walked, Shane asked, "Are you going to have to put Gavin on the stand?"

"Only if I absolutely have to," Jason replied. "Right now, I don't have anyone to tell his side of the story, to testify to the real nature of their relationship. Unfortunately, Gavin doesn't have a lot of close friends and any he does have are closer to Alison, so they've turned their backs on him."

"If you let Gavin testify, he doesn't exactly ooze sincerity," Shane said.

"I know," Jason said with a sigh. "It's just the way he is and my fear is the jury will take it as indifference to Paige's death and a sign of guilt."

"It's going to be a tough call for you," Shane said.

"You need to find me something or someone to counter the Crown's case, the sooner the better," Jason said, looking at Shane as they walked.

"I'm trying," Shane responded. "If someone other than Benton murdered Paige, we know it was personal given how she was assaulted. It means that someone took their anger out on Paige, either to punish her for getting involved with Gavin or to make her suffer as a way of hurting Gavin."

"The question is whether there's anyone involved in this case that fits that description," Jason said.

"It's a question that right now, I don't have an answer to," Shane said.

Chapter Eight - Present

Emma looked around her crowded kitchen and seriously thought about going to her bedroom, closing the door, and giving herself some personal space so she could take a few calming breaths and think.

She had driven to the Brantford Police Station and reported Shane missing, which got an immediate response from officers with the Service's Missing Persons Unit. A plainclothes Sergeant and a Constable took her to an interview room for a detailed report, asking personal questions about Shane and his work, his state of mind in the time period leading up to his disappearance, any problems he might have been having, including with drugs or alcohol, had he ever gone out of touch before, and even if there were any difficulties in their relationship. Emma tried to remain calm and not get irritated by the questions because she knew they were just doing their jobs.

Jason arrived at the station and was allowed to join Emma in the interview room where he answered questions about the nature of Shane's work for him, what he was currently working on, and if he was aware of any threats Shane had received. An alert had been sent out to all of the cruisers currently on patrol to keep an eye out for Shane's Charger and a forensic team was sent to search the parking area behind Burke and Associates in case there were any signs of a struggle. Emma explained that she had been texting and calling Shane's cellphone, and had left numerous messages, but now either his phone's battery had died or the phone was turned off. The 'Find a Phone' feature on Emma's cell couldn't ping a location for Shane's and the police had no luck using the resources at their disposal, including having Shane's service provider trace the location of his last call, which turned out to be his office. It appeared there was a good chance that Shane's phone had been smashed or at least the SIM card removed and destroyed.

Emma and Jason, who had cleared his normally busy calendar, were at the police station for over two hours answering questions and waiting for long periods while the police organized their search strategy. Once the initial questioning was completed, Emma thought the time was right, and she told Sergeant Raymond Lucas, head of the Missing Person's Unit, that it was possible Shane's disappearance was linked to her foster child, Lan, and her possible testimony against the head of a Vietnamese-Canadian criminal organization.

"You perhaps should have told me this right at the start," Lucas said. Lucas was in his mid-forties, a trim black man with a bushy moustache.

"I'm sorry, I just didn't want to sound an alarm that probably isn't there," Emma responded.

"But you think it's possible Shane was taken as leverage to get Lan not to testify," Lucas said and then added, "To be honest, that sounds like it would be a rather bold and desperate move on their part."

"I know, that's why I was hesitant to suggest it," Emma said, "But I do think the RCMP should be informed just in case. I can give you the name of the officer heading the investigation."

Emma then got Sergeant Gurdeep Singh's card out of her purse and gave it to Lucas who wrote the information on his notepad. He then got up and left the interview room.

After the two hours had passed at the police station and there were no leads to Shane's whereabouts, Emma asked to go home to wait for any word, to be there in case Shane showed up, and to be there when Lan came home from school.

Now, Emma was in her kitchen, thinking about getting away for a few minutes, and listening to the chatter from the two men and one woman standing nearby. Sergeant Lucas was there along with one of the officers from his unit, Constable Laurie Liss, probably because Emma would appreciate having another woman to talk to. Also in the room was Sergeant Singh, who had driven down from his office in Hamilton as soon as he was contacted. Singh told Lucas he was only there to observe and be on standby if it turned out the Vietnamese-Canadian gang was involved.

"I think if Hong Phuong's people kidnapped Shane, they would have been in contact by now," Emma heard Singh tell Lucas and Liss.

Emma's phone was sitting on the kitchen table so she could put it on speaker if a call came in. Everything was in place to start an immediate trace if there was a call about Shane and Constable Liss was holding a phone that had been mirrored to Emma's and would record any conversations.

Jason, who had been in the living room making calls to his various contacts in case someone had heard from Shane, walked into the kitchen and said, "I just got word on something that could possibly be linked to Shane's disappearance. Gavin Benson has committed suicide in his cell at Millhaven."

"This is the man from the last major case Shane worked on that you and Emma told me about," Lucas stated.

"Yes," Jason replied and then turned to Emma and said, "I'm sorry Emma, I need to go to the office because there are several things I will need to handle."

"It's not a problem, Jason, I really appreciate you being here for me," Emma said. "I'll call if I hear anything."

"I think we have to shift our investigation into a possible link between Benson's death and Shane's disappearance," Lucas said. "I'm going to have one of my officers pull the files on the Madison murder and Jason, can you or your staff give us access to the information you have on the people involved in the trial so we can trace their current whereabouts?"

"Whatever you need," Jason answered and Lucas left the kitchen to make some calls.

Jason made his way to the front door and Emma went with him. When they got there, Emma embraced Jason and he could feel her tears on the side of his neck.

"I'm desperately trying to stay calm and positive, but I can't stop myself from thinking that Shane is probably dead," she said softly. "He's made enemies when he's solved cases."

They stepped apart and Jason fished a tissue out of the pocket of his suit jacket and gave it to Emma to wipe her eyes. "He's not dead, Emma," Jason said. "I'm convinced he's been kidnapped and is being held somewhere for a reason we don't know yet. Once we do, we'll get him back, you'll see."

Jason left, Emma did her best to compose herself and then returned to the kitchen where she busied herself making more coffee. She had just reset the coffeemaker when the doorbell chimed and when she opened the front door, she was greeted by Ben Chen standing on the front step along with a woman she didn't know.

"Ben, you're here! You didn't need to come," Emma said, realizing that with everything that was going on, she had forgotten she called Ben to ask if he had heard from Shane. Ben had said he was on his way and then hung up before Emma could respond.

"Are you fucking kidding me!? My best fucking friend, well actually my only friend, is missing and there's no fucking way I'm not coming to help find him and support you!" Ben exclaimed.

"Come in, come in! I am glad you're here," Emma responded, trying to sound enthused, and stepped back from the threshold to let Ben and his female companion in. It was not that Emma didn't like Ben, she did, and she knew under all of his inappropriate comments and his inability to talk without foul language, he had a big heart and was secretly a very generous contributor to his community. But the sick jokes and the bad language often got under Emma's skin.

As soon as he was in the door, Ben grabbed Emma in a bear hug, his arms around her waist and the top of his head just below Emma's chin because he was so much shorter than her.

"We're going to find him, Emma, safe and alive," Ben declared and then turned to the woman with him and said, "Emma, this is my friend, Michelle Watson."

Michelle was slightly taller than Ben and rail thin, with long dark hair parted in the middle, framing a pale face with a petite nose featuring three small rings through the right nostril, green eyes, long fake lashes, thick black eyeliner, dark purple eye shadow and at least half a dozen rings down the outside of each ear. She was wearing a waist-length leather jacket, blue jeans and a white t-shirt with 'Bullshit Baffles Brains' in bold letters on the front.

Emma smiled and said, "I've heard a lot about you, Michelle, through Shane, and I'm glad to finally meet you in person."

Michelle stepped forward, gave Emma a quick hug, and said, "I'm glad to finally meet you too, Emma, but I sure wish it was under better fucking circumstances. I'm so sorry about what's going on with Shane. I only met him once, but he's a great fucking guy and Benny thinks the world of him."

Benny? Shane had told her that's what Michelle called Ben and, like Shane, she couldn't believe that Ben would allow anyone to do that. Shane had also told her that Ben's girlfriend confirmed that opposites do sometimes attract, although they both did like to swear a lot.

"Come on to the kitchen, I just made some coffee," Emma said and then added, "There are a couple of police officers here."

"We'll try to stay out of the fucking way and I'll try not to be an asshole and irritate them," Ben said.

That's not going to happen, Emma thought, and then asked, "You two want to stay at the house? I'm sure I can find some room."

"No, I already booked us a room at a motel on Fairview Street," Ben said and then added, "Emma, I know the police are on it, but I'm going to do whatever it fucking takes to find Shane. I brought Michelle with me because she's super smart and has even better computer skills than me. We're going to deep dive the internet in case there is any chatter about Shane and hack our fucking way into every available surveillance camera in case we can spot the Charger parked somewhere."

"Thanks, I appreciate the help," Emma said sincerely. Just as they were about to enter the kitchen, Emma stopped, turned and said, "I just wanted to mention that my foster daughter, Lan, will be home soon."

"I can hardly wait to finally meet her," Ben said enthusiastically.

"Fuck, yeah, me too! Ben says she's super smart," Michelle added.

"Well, I'm wondering if you would do me a favour," Emma continued. "Lan is highly intelligent, but she's still only nine years old, and while I'm sure she's heard lots of swear words, including from me and Shane, I don't think it's a good idea for her to hear 'fuck' in every sentence. It would give her the wrong idea about what's appropriate. I personally don't care, and I'm sorry for asking, but could you and Michelle try and keep your language under control when she's around?"

"No need to apologize, Emma, we understand," Ben responded. "You can fucking count on us. Oh, sorry, that slipped."

Emma did her best to smile at Shane's well meaning best friend. She knew that Ben would put everything he had into finding Shane and if nothing else, his being here was a welcome distraction from the dark, painful thoughts she was having.

Shane's not dead! she told herself.

He's been kidnapped for some demand we don't know yet, or he's been badly injured somehow and can't get in contact.

Where are you, Shane?

Chapter Nine

Shane was exhausted, his eyes were burning, his butt hurt from sitting on the concrete floor, and his damaged left knee was making its presence felt even more than normal.

His watch had been taken when he was kidnapped, so Shane had no idea what time it was or how long he had been studying the transcripts from the Benson trial, but he knew he had been at it for hours. Shortly after he had started reading, Josh had opened the trap in the door and dropped another bottle of water through the opening onto the floor, followed by a pad of paper and a pen. Shane tried to speak to him, but Josh didn't respond and quickly closed the trap. Over a dozen pages of the pad were now filled with notes, but Shane acknowledged to himself that so far, they were just random thoughts that did little in the way of suggesting possible leads to someone else, rather than Gavin Benson, being responsible for the murder of Paige Madison.

On two different occasions when a blurry eyed Shane started to fall asleep, the ear-piercing music and bright lights started up, and he went down into the fetal position on the floor, eyes jammed shut and fingers in his ears until it stopped. The torture felt like it went on for hours and Shane knew it was a reminder from Josh of the consequences of not concentrating on his father's case.

Josh was obviously monitoring Shane from a tiny remote camera hidden somewhere in the room and it was further proof to Shane that his abductor was more than just an ordinary soldier with the Canadian Forces. He was knowledgeable about the advanced interrogation techniques used at so-called 'black sites' where members of intelligence agencies took prisoners, often suspected terrorists. Josh had access to psychedelic drugs used for the same purpose and specialized equipment. He was waiting in the back seat of the Charger to inject Shane with a fast-acting tranquillizer, a car in which Shane had installed a high-end security system. Josh must have had some kind of device that scanned the car and found the frequency used by the fob that Shane carried to disarm the alarm.

Shane set the transcript aside and leaned his head against the wall to take a mental break but he didn't dare close his eyes in case Josh was still monitoring him and decided to give him another dose of the lights and music. He looked down at his left knee and tried to will away the throbbing pain that had been his companion for so long. The knee had been severely damaged when Shane was a rookie with the Brantford Police Service and attended a domestic dispute with his training officer, Charlie Oak, who was now the Police Chief. A heavily intoxicated man shot Oak, who was saved by his bullet-proof vest, and then turned his shotgun on his also intoxicated wife whom Shane was propping up. Shane pushed the woman to the floor, saving her life, but the shotgun slug hit his left kneecap, destroying the joint. Shane underwent multiple surgeries and received an artificial kneecap, but he was left with a permanent limp and required the use of a cane. He suffered constant pain in the knee, which some doctors told him was psychosomatic, but it was very real to him.

As Shane looked at his knee, he instinctively reached out to ensure his cane was beside him, but remembered he didn't have his constant companion, nor did he have the non-addictive pain medication he took on a daily basis. There was a plan for Shane to receive a new type of total knee replacement, not possible before because of the severe damage to the bone and muscle structure above and below his knee. But when Shane met with the orthopedic surgeon in Toronto who had pioneered the procedure, it was decided he should wait a few more years because he was still young, the artificial knee had a limited life span, and a second replacement might not be possible, which would mean an amputation. Shane told the surgeon that if amputation of his leg from above the knee down was an inevitability, then it might as well be done now so he would be free of the constant pain. That option was still on the table the last time he met with the specialist.

Shane picked up the pad of paper and started leafing through the pages of notes he had made while reading the trial transcript, but there was nothing that caught his attention. The Crown's theory, which the jury agreed with, was that Gavin Benson was lying when he claimed he didn't know Paige was pregnant, that he was in love with Paige and planned to leave his wife so he could marry her. Instead, the Crown claimed that Benson considered his affair with Paige as nothing more than the opportunity to have sex with a much younger, beautiful woman, and he was stringing her along with his promises of a permanent relationship. When Benton's partner threatened his position in the company over the affair and then Paige told him she was pregnant and threatened to talk to his wife, he snapped, strangled Paige, violated her, and then dumped her body in a field in an attempt to make it look like someone else was responsible.

Jason did his usual masterful job in trying to put reasonable doubt in the minds of the jurors, but it fell short and although Jason adamantly refused to accept it, Shane did blame himself for not finding more ammunition for the lawyer to use. Other people who would have had the motive to kill Paige had what appeared to be air-tight alibis for the time of the murder, including Gavin's wife, Alison, who insisted she was completely unaware her husband was having an affair. Shane, with researcher Chioma Abiola's help, dug deep into Alison's life looking for some indication she was lying and Chioma even illegally hacked Alison's bank records looking for a possible payoff to someone else to kill Paige. They did the same thing with Gavin's daughter, Melissa Edwards and her husband Jake, but there was nothing. Gavin's partner, Ethan Holdaway, was at home with his wife and then in the office during the period during which the murder occurred and there was no provable gap between the two.

Her best friend, Ariel Durst, insisted that Paige had not been involved romantically with anyone else for at least a year prior to her starting her affair with Benton and was instead working long hours and staying home. Shane tracked down and talked to several of Paige's other friends and they said the same thing. It ruled out the possibility of a jealous ex-boyfriend.

After looking at his notes and thinking about the various people in Paige's life, Shane turned his attention to his abductor, Gavin's son, Josh Benson. He understood Josh's anger over his father's suicide because he believed his dad was innocent, but why was he willing to throw his own life away by abducting Shane and trying to force him to find someone else responsible for his sister's murder? It was an extreme reaction and while Shane was trying hard not to think about it, there was a real possibility that he was not going to leave this room alive. Kidnapping was one thing, but Josh had to know that if he killed Shane, he would be eventually caught and spend the rest of his life in prison. What if this abduction was really about guilt? What if it was Josh who killed Paige and believed his father would be found innocent and he would get away with murder? But that didn't happen, his father was found guilty and then took his own life. Josh is wracked with guilt, but rather than simply confess, his disturbed mind decides he should be punished further by kidnapping Shane and making him conclude that Josh killed his sister.

Prior to the trial, Shane confirmed that Josh was on base at Borden at the time of the murder and the security gate log showed he had made no entries or exists. But if Josh was, as Shane suspected, some type of military intelligence operative, getting around the gate log, which was likely stored on a computer, wouldn't be a problem for him. If Josh was able to get his hands on the electronic equipment and drugs he was using on Shane without raising a red flag at Borden, then covering his whereabouts when Paige was murdered wouldn't be a problem.

Do I confront Josh with my theory next time he opens the trap door? Shane asked himself. If I push him, will he admit that I'm right and that he kidnapped me so that I would conclude he was the killer? This whole situation made no sense to Shane but probably did to a guilt ridden Josh if he's suffered some kind of mental breakdown. And when I tell Josh what he wants to hear, what then? Shane wondered. Will he simply open the door and let me go so that I can go to the police and have him arrested? Shane thought it was more likely that Josh, after being told what he wanted to hear, would kill him and then cover his tracks.

Somehow, I need to find a way to get out of here, Shane concluded.

Chapter Ten - The Trial

"The Crown calls Ethan Holdaway to the stand," Prosecutor Evan Gregory announced and Gavin Benson's business partner stood up from his spot on the courtroom's public benches and made his way to the witness chair to the left of Judge Garnet.

Holdaway was the physical opposite of Benson's distinguished good looks; he was short at only five foot seven inches tall, medium built with a paunch hanging over the belt of the suit pants he was wearing, a pale round face, brown eyes under bushy eyebrows, thinning brown and gray hair, and stylish frame-less glasses.

After being sworn in, Holdaway sat, unbuttoned the jacket of the dark blue suit he was wearing, crossed his legs, clasped his hands on his lap and put a slight smile on his face. He's trying to look casual and in control, Jason Burke thought as he studied Holdaway from his chair at the defence table. The posture was likely suggested by the Prosecutor, Jason concluded, because Holdaway was one of the Crown's key witnesses and they didn't want him looking nervous and tentative to the jury.

"Mr. Holdaway," Gregory began, "You and the defendant have been partners in Grand River Associates for a long time."

"Yes, over twenty years," Holdaway replied. "Gavin and I met at university, we became good friends and decided to start our own engineering firm."

"So you know the defendant really well, you have a close personal relationship," Gregory stated.

"We're not as close as we once were because we both have families and very busy lives," Holdaway said.

"How did you become aware that the defendant and Paige Madison were involved in a relationship?" Gregory asked.

"It wasn't just one thing, it was a number of things," Holdaway replied. "Gavin hadn't bothered with Paige very much around the office and then suddenly he was spending a lot of time standing at her desk talking to her or they would have coffee together in the break room and they were holding closed-door meetings in his office."

"All this time together wasn't because she was helping him with a project?" Gregory asked.

"No, that was not the nature of Paige's job. She strictly handled clerical work," Holdaway said.

"Was there any incident that confirmed your suspicion they were romantically involved"? Gregory asked.

"I had left the office to go home and Gavin and Paige were still there," Holdaway said. "I realized I had forgotten some plans I would need for an early morning meeting the next day at a construction site, so I went back into the office using the door at the back of the building which doesn't sound a chime like the front door when it's opened. When I walked by Gavin's office on the way to mine, his door was opened and I could see him and Paige embracing and kissing. He had his hands all over her."

"They didn't see you," Gregory stated.

"No, they were too busy with what they were doing," Holdaway responded and his answer set off the sound of people on the visitor's benches whispering and some were giggling.

Judge Garnet tapped his gavel and with a scowl on his face said, "I'll have none of that in my courtroom or I will ask everyone to leave." He then turned to the Prosecutor and said, "Please continue, Mr. Gregory."

"When did you confront Mr. Benton about the situation?" Gregory asked Holdaway.

"The next morning," Holdaway responded. "I called Gavin into my office, told him what I saw, that it was unacceptable behaviour and reminded him that he was a married man. I also told him that he was exposing us to all kinds of possible legal and financial problems if Paige decided she no longer wanted his advances. She could accuse him of sexual harassment, he could be charged and even if he was found not guilty, his reputation and the firm's reputation would be ruined. It was also possible Paige could decide to sue us."

"And what was the defendant's reaction?" Gregory asked.

"He got angry right away, which was not a surprise because Gavin always had a bit of a hair trigger and it never took much to set him off," Holdaway said. "First, he told me his personal life was none of my business and when I told him something like this going on in the office between a boss and an employee was my business, he insisted I was making too big a deal out of the whole thing. He insisted the kiss was a spur of the moment thing which he regretted. I told him there was a lot more than just kissing going on and that he was fondling Paige."

"And what did he say about that?" Gregory asked.

"He said Paige was the aggressor and that she had been pursuing a relationship with him for some time," Holdaway replied and then added, "He said he finally gave into temptation and was sorry it happened and had told Paige that."

"So, the defendant didn't say to you, 'I love her' or 'I want to be with her' or 'I'm going to leave my wife for her', anything like that?" Gregory stated.

"No, he just kept calling it a mistake," Holdaway responded.

"Mr. Holdaway, did you threaten to dissolve your partnership with the defendant if he didn't immediately end the affair with Paige and find a legitimate reason for her to leave the company," Gregory asked.

"I did," Holdaway said in a firm voice. "I needed Gavin to understand just how serious the legal and financial consequences could be of an older man, in a position of authority, having sex with a much younger employee."

"And now did the defendant react?" Gregory asked.

"He got very angry and upset, and again blamed Paige for what happened," Holdaway said.

"He say anything else?" Gregory prompted.

"He said, 'I'll take care of it, she won't be a problem'," Holdaway responded.

Gregory looked at the jury to add dramatic effect to the witness's statement, then turned back to Holdaway and asked, "That's exactly what the defendant said? 'I'll take care of it, she won't be a problem'?"

"Yes," Holdaway stated in response.

"Did the tone of the defendant's response concern you?" Gregory asked.

"Absolutely!" Holdaway said. "As I said, Gavin was very angry and I became worried about what his response might be."

At the defence table, Gavin suddenly jumped to his feet and yelled, "That's bullshit, Ethan, and you know it! Why are you doing this!? You're supposed to be my friend!"

Benson's outburst caused a noisy stir in the courtroom. Jason stood up, took Gavin by the arm and pulled him back down onto his chair. Judge Garnet, meantime, banged his gavel loudly several times and said, "Mr. Benson, you will control yourself and keep your comments to yourself! Another outburst and I won't hesitate to have you watch the rest of your trial on closed-circuit TV in your jail cell."

Jason stood up and said, "Mr. Benson understands and apologizes to the court."

"Make sure he does, Mr. Burke," Garnet responded sternly and then, turning toward the Prosecutor, said, "You may continue, Mr. Gregory."

Gregory, with a self-satisfied look on his face, said, "I'm finished with this witness, your Honour, and yield to my honourable colleague."

"Thank you, Mr. Gregory. You may proceed with the witness, Mr. Burke," Judge Garnet said.

Jason was always impressed that no matter what happened, decorum always ruled in Canadian courts, which were modeled on the British system, right down to the often hot and uncomfortable suits and cloaks worn by lawyers. One of the noticeable differences was that lawyers in Supreme Court cases in Canada no longer wore the wigs still used in Britain.

Jason stood up, walked around to the front of the defence table, and said, "Mr. Holdaway, are you suggesting to this court that when my client said, 'I'll take care of it, she won't be a problem', you immediately believed he meant he was going to brutally assault Paige Madison and choke her to death?"

"Well, no," Holdaway started but before he went any further, Jason asked, "So, what did you think he meant by that?"

"Well, I suppose I assumed he meant he would talk to her," Holdaway stammered.

"You suppose, or you know?" Jason quickly asked. "You knew the guy for over twenty years, you must have known what he meant."

"Well, I did, but...," Holdaway started to say, but Jason again jumped in before he went any further and said, "Okay, so we've established that you and the Prosecutor created a false impression for the jury by suggesting that when my client said to you, 'I'll take care of it, she won't be a problem', that he was saying he planned to harm Ms. Madison."

Gregory then stood up and said, "Your Honour, shouldn't Mr. Holdaway be allowed to complete what he was saying without being interrupted by my colleague, who I suggest is badgering the witness."

"Badgering?" Jason responded, "I'm just trying to help this witness clarify the false impression you helped him create about my client's intentions toward Ms. Madison."

"Okay, that's enough," Judge Garnet admonished. "We've had good decorum so far in this trial, so let's not ruin that. Mr. Burke, I would tend to agree with the Prosecutor that you are cutting the witness off before he's had a chance to complete his answer."

"I apologize, your Honour," Jason said. "I'm done with that line of questioning anyway."

"Very well, but remember what I just said," Garnet said.

Jason turned back to the witness box and asked, "Mr. Holdaway, how well did you know Ms. Madison?"

"I didn't know anything about her personal life if that's what you're asking," Holdaway said. "Gavin was responsible for the hiring and supervising of staff, and my only day-to-day contact with Paige was when I asked her to perform some clerical work for me."

"But you obviously kept a close eye on what she was up to if, as you told the Prosecutor, you noticed my client was spending a lot of time with her," Jason stated.

"Well, no, I wasn't going out of my way to keep an eye on her," Holdaway answered in a defensive tone. "As I said, my only direct contact with Paige was when I was discussing whatever she was working on for me."

"But, for some reason, you thought it was unusual that Paige was spending so much time with my client, even though he was in charge of the work performed by the office staff and was her direct supervisor," Jason said, putting some skepticism in his voice. "I know you said you weren't purposely watching Ms. Madison, but was my client the only male on staff she hung around with?"

"Well, no," Holdaway answered. "Quite frankly, one of the main reasons Paige's relationship with Gavin caught my attention was because she was always flirting with the men on staff."

Holdaway shifted nervously in his chair and then said, "Out of respect for Paige and because of her tragic death, I was really hoping

I wouldn't have to mention this, but she was a beautiful young woman and she knew it, and it seemed to me she was using that fact to ingratiate herself with the men on staff in order to advance her position with the company."

"That's an interesting allegation about Ms. Madison that you've suddenly decided to share," Jason said and then asked, "Did she flirt with you?"

"Your Honour!" Gregory exclaimed as he stood up from his chair. "I fail to see the relevance of this question. Mr. Holdaway is here to testify about his discovery of the affair between Mr. Benson and Ms. Madison, and Mr. Benson's reaction."

Before Jason could respond, Judge Garnet put up his hand to stop him and said, "I think this line of questioning is very relevant. I think the jury should have as clear a picture as possible of the circumstances leading up to the confrontation between Mr. Holdaway and Mr. Benson about the affair."

Garnet then turned in his chair to face the witness box and said, "Please answer the question, Mr. Holdaway."

"No, she did not," Holdaway said firmly. "I think she realized that I would not put up with that kind of thing."

"Were you put out, maybe a bit jealous that she didn't give you a little attention?" Jason asked.

"Your Honour!" Gregory complained but before he could go any further, Judge Garnet again put his hand up and said, "Please move on, Mr. Burke."

"Certainly, Your Honour," Jason said and then asked Holdaway, "Wasn't it a bit extreme threatening to dissolve your company over an office affair?"

"I actually said I would dissolve our partnership, not the business," Holdaway responded. "I needed Gavin to understand that if his involvement with Paige ended badly, I would be forced to distance myself from him in order to save the company."

"I don't suppose you were using the affair as a way of walking away scot-free from a company in serious financial trouble, leaving your partner, my client, holding the bag?" Jason asked with an accusatory tone in his voice.

"Your Honour," Gregory stood up and said before Holdaway could answer. "Mr. Burke is asking about something that has not been introduced to this trial as a fact and is therefore not relevant."

"Your Honour," Jason said as he stepped over to the defence table and held up a small stack of documents. "If the court wishes, I can introduce into evidence financial documents supplied by my client which show Grand River Associates was carrying a debt of over two million dollars and its current revenue was down forty percent compared to the previous year."

"Your Honour, the defence did not make these documents available to the Crown before the trial, therefore they are inadmissible and any questions related to them should not be allowed," Gregory countered.

"I would tend to agree," Judge Garnet said.

Jason noted to himself that Garnet used the phrase 'I tend to agree' a lot, suggesting he was not very decisive with his in-trial rulings. Jason hoped that would be the case now.

"Your Honour, through the Prosecutor's questions of Mr. Holdaway, the Crown is contending that his threat of dissolving the partnership, and in effect the company, over my client's affair, was a motive for my client killing Ms. Madison," Jason said. "The Prosecutor introduced discussion about the business to the trial, not the defence, and we should be allowed to counter anything said about it."

"My colleague would have been well aware this line of questioning would occur because it was discussed during the mandatory pretrial conference and was part of the preliminary hearing," Gregory countered. "So, if he planned to refute it during cross-examination, he should have disclosed his evidence."

"Your Honour, as you are aware, Canada does not have legislated defence disclosure rules, leaving previous common law rulings, which I am prepared to argue," Jason said. "But I think this falls under the accused's strict right not to reveal his defence until the

Crown's case is presented. I would further argue that it was up to the Crown to do its due diligence on the financial state of his company before allowing Mr. Holdaway to suggest in his testimony that the affair between my client and Ms. Madison would be the sole reason he would dissolve the partnership. The Prosecutor knew or should have known, about the troubled finances. He opened this door and we should be able to counter it, with documentation."

"I would tend to agree," Judge Garnet said and Jason forced himself not to smile. "I could call an adjournment while this disclosure question is settled, but there would be no point since Mr. Burke, rightly or wrongly, has already presented his document in front of the jury. I'm going to allow the financial statements into evidence for the purpose of cross-examination of the witness about his testimony while being questioned by the Prosecutor."

"I would request that my objection be put on the record," Gregory stated.

"So noted," Garnet said.

Jason knew Gregory wanted his objection on file just in case Benson was found not guilty and he needed a cause for an appeal.

"You may continue, Mr. Burke," Garnet said.

Jason turned to the witness stand and said, "So, Mr. Holdaway, returning to my question, did the affair not give you a good excuse to walk away from your failing company?"

Jason saw and hoped the jury noticed that Holdaway was getting uncomfortable, moving around in his chair and unclasping and clasping his hands on his lap.

"Well, um…," Holdaway started and then stopped to clear his throat before continuing. "The company's finances would've been in the back of my mind at the time, not because I wanted out, but because Gavin's affair could put a recovery in serious jeopardy."

"But wouldn't you agree that you were wrong to try and leave the impression that you had this great, successful engineering firm and that you threatened to dissolve your partnership with my client solely because of his affair?" Jason asked.

"It was not my intent to leave that impression…," Holdaway started but Jason interrupted by saying in an aggressive tone, "Well it sure sounded like it."

Jason looked at the jury briefly then turned to the Judge and said, "I am finished questioning this witness, your Honour," before returning to his table.

Judge Garnet adjourned the trial for the day and Jason met with Gavin in a small interview room on the same floor as the courthouse prisoner holding cells. Gavin was visibly upset and was pacing back and forth until Jason convinced him to calm down and sit.

"My supposed friend and partner is trying to screw me!" Gavin exclaimed.

"I know it's upsetting, but getting angry in court doesn't help," Jason said. "All it does is demonstrate to the jury that you have a hair-trigger temper and suggests that maybe you lost your temper with Paige and killed her."

"I need to testify. I need to tell the jury how much I loved Paige and about our plans for the future," Gavin said pleadingly.

"It may come to that, but most of the time it's not a good idea for the defendant in a murder trial to take the stand in their own defence," Jason said. "The Prosecutor will question you aggressively and you might not come across as credible to the jury. For example, although he didn't tell the whole story about your conversation, you did, at first, tell Holdaway that your affair with Paige was meaningless and that she was the aggressor. Correct?"

"I did that hoping that Evan would accept the explanation and let it go," Gavin said. "If he believed I put a stop to it, there would be no issue and Paige and I would just have to be a lot more careful about our interactions in the office."

"But then Evan started going on about possible legal issues and threatened our partnership, so I told him the truth, that Paige and I were deeply in love and planned to be together. But he didn't accept that. He didn't say anything about that in court."

"But if you get on the stand, I can guarantee you the Prosecutor will grill you about your two different stories to Holdaway and suggest your claims about the nature of your relationship with Paige are not believable," Jason explained.

"But we need to do something!" Gavin pleaded. "The jury already has the impression that I killed Paige because she got pregnant and threatened to ruin my life."

"Gavin, at this point, our best strategy continues to be establishing reasonable doubt," Jason said and then thought to himself that the hill to doing that continued to get a lot steeper.

Chapter Eleven - Present

Emma looked at the illuminated numbers on her bedside clock radio and realized her attempt to get more than a couple of hours of sleep wasn't going to work.

She had finally succumbed to her physical and mental exhaustion at 1 am and stretched out on her bed without undressing, but as soon as she closed her eyes thoughts of Shane lying dead somewhere brought tears to her eyes and an anguish she couldn't set aside long enough to fall asleep. After tossing and turning for what seemed like hours, she finally fell asleep only to come fully awake and see 3 am on the clock.

As each hour went by and no kidnapper made contact, Emma's mantra to herself and everyone around her that Shane was taken by someone and was still alive was fading to the reality of the situation. The police officers assigned to the case kept telling her not to lose hope and that they were working on the assumption that Shane was alive, but Emma could tell by the look in their eyes that they believed otherwise. As well, even though she had not been officially told, by the time she went to try and get some sleep the number of officers assigned to investigate Shane's disappearance and search for his Charger had been substantially reduced. Shane had a lot of friends on the Brantford Police Service and with the local OPP

Detachment and she suspected no one wanted to be the one to tell her the situation had moved to a wait for a body to be found.

Emma got up from her bed, went into the bathroom, used the toilet, and splashed some water on her face. After drying off, she looked at her reflection in the mirror above the sink and thought that Shane, who was always telling her how beautiful she was, wouldn't think that if he could see her now. Her short blonde hair was tangled and sticking up in some places, her blue eyes were bloodshot and her normally soft unblemished complexion was dry and pale. The lines beside Emma's eyes that had developed over the years looked like deep crevices and the fine lines on each side of her lips, normally covered by makeup were more visible than ever.

Emma told herself that when they find Shane she will apply some makeup so she'll look nice when he gets home and then left the bathroom and walked down the hall to the kitchen where she saw the light was on. When she entered, Ben Chen and his girlfriend, Michelle, were still at the kitchen table where she left them when she went to try and get some sleep. She expected them to look haggard and tired, but they looked surprisingly fresh and were both working on the laptops on the table in front of them with the same intensity they had many hours before.

"Ben, you and Michelle need to take a break and get some rest or you'll burn yourself out," Emma said.

"No fucking way!" Ben exclaimed without looking up from his laptop. "I'm not stopping until I find some kind of clue to where Shane is. He'd do the same fucking thing for me."

Ben then looked over at his girlfriend beside him and said, "Michelle, maybe you should get some rest."

"Fuck rest," Michelle responded. "Let's keep at it. Maybe Emma will make some more of her great coffee"

"Yeah, I can do that, I need some myself," Emma said and walked over to the counter to get the container of ground coffee from one of the cupboards. "Are you guys having any luck?" she asked.

"We're working on two things," Ben responded. "I've been searching social media and the dark web looking for any recent mention of Shane's name, perhaps a threatening or angry post aimed at him, but so far, fucking nothing. You told police the Benson murder trial was the last big case that Shane worked on and there are a ton of fucking posts about that, but most are aimed at Benson and how the jury was right to find the asshole guilty. We know that Shane would have worked in the background so it's no surprise that he's never mentioned."

"If Shane was kidnapped, it could be related to any one of several sensitive cases he's worked on," Emma said, the exasperation evident in her voice.

"Michelle is working on a different strategy," Ben continued. "If we can find Shane's fucking car, then maybe we can find him."

Ben explained that several offices and businesses in the area around Burke and Associates on King Street have security cameras on their front entrance. While many only focus on a narrow area at the front door, some have a wide-angle lens and show the traffic on the street. Michelle was trying to locate those cameras and then hack into them, hoping the video was being saved on at least a twenty four hour loop.

"If we can pick up at least one image of the Charger, then we'll know exactly which way it was travelling during the time period Shane disappeared," Michelle said, not taking her eyes off the monitor of her laptop and typing furiously on the keyboard.

Ben then told Emma that like many cities, Brantford will have a series of web-cams at multiple locations, used primarily to show weather conditions. The images might not be saved to a file, but it will be worth the effort to hack into the websites that host the cams just in case. Ben also explained that Ontario's 511 weather and traffic service has over 800 cameras along major highways and the Compass System has over 200 cameras.

"We're going to search any stored data we can find along Highway 403," Ben said. "I'm not sure, but I think the Compass System keeps images for something like fifteen days and you have to make a Freedom of Information request to get them. But fuck that, we don't have time, I'll find a way to access them."

"Ben, please don't be doing anything illegal," Emma said. "I don't want to see you and Michelle in legal trouble, I've got enough to deal with."

Ben was about to answer but he spotted someone standing behind Emma and said, "Hey there, Miss Lan."

Emma turned and saw Lan standing just inside the entrance to the kitchen, wearing white pyjamas with Harry Potter images and rubbing her eyes to adjust to the light.

"Lan, what are you doing up? It's very early in the morning and you should still be asleep," Emma said.

"I woke up and heard voices and I thought maybe Shane was home," Lan said.

"No sweetie, Shane's not home yet, we're still looking for him," Emma said softly. "You need to go back to bed and get some more sleep. It's a school day."

"Don't you worry, Miss Lan, Ben Chen is on the fucking case and he's going to find Shane," Ben stated.

"Ben, language," Emma admonished.

"Sorry, it slipped," Ben said.

"It's okay, Emma, I've heard that word lots of times. It doesn't bother me. The boys at school use the 'F' word all the time," Lan said with a smile on her face.

"That's fine, but you don't need to also hear it at home," Emma said. "Now, head back to bed."

"Okay. Goodnight Ben, goodnight Michelle," Lan said.

Michelle was concentrating intensely on her laptop and didn't respond, but Ben said, "Have a good sleep, Miss Lan and sorry about using the word 'fuck', I mean the 'F' word. Sorry, Emma."

"Christ, Ben," Emma responded and they could hear Lan giggling as she walked down the hall to her bedroom.

"Okay, I got the Charger!" Michelle suddenly said excitingly.

Ben got up from his chair and Emma stepped over and they both stood behind Michelle looking over her shoulders. On her laptop was a screen capture looking down on a street and in it an overhead shot of a black car.

"That's fucking it!" Ben exclaimed. "Even overhead you can't miss the distinctive lines of a classic Dodge Charger. Way to go Michelle! You fucking rock!"

"Keep your voice down, Ben, Lan's probably still awake," Emma admonished but her heart started beating faster with excitement.

"I got more," Michelle continued. "This shot was captured by a traffic camera on a street light on Colborne Street shortly after noon, the period during which Shane was last seen when he left his office for lunch. From there, I figured the car would either continue on Colborne Street East out of the city or turn onto the Wayne Gretzky Parkway heading northbound, either that way out of Brantford or to the ramps for Highway 403. I decided to start with the Parkway and got lucky. One of the cameras at a gas bar at the Henry Street intersection that is supposed to monitor the pumps somehow got knocked out of position and hasn't been fixed so most of it's pointing toward the Parkway."

Michelle changed the screen on her laptop and there was a shot of a distinctive black car sitting between an SUV and a van at the stoplight.

"Can you see who's driving?" Emma asked, the anticipation obvious in her voice.

"I'm sorry, no," Michelle said as she increased the magnification on the image. Each time she got closer to the Charger, the image got blurrier and the pixilation bigger. "It's not a high-end camera and it's too far away," Michelle added.

"Fuck. But it's the Charger," Ben said.

"I figured it was heading for the highway, so I started searching screenshots from both the eastbound and westbound 403 around the same time and I found this eastbound," Michelle said as she pulled up an image of the Charger in the driving lane. "Again, you can't see who's driving but you can tell there's only one person in the car."

"So that's either Shane heading somewhere he didn't tell anyone about, or someone else is driving and Shane is either lying down in the back seat or is in the trunk," Emma said.

"Fuck, Michelle, I'm good, but I don't think I could've found this," Ben said.

"Thanks. I'm still searching along the highway between Brantford and Hamilton, but so far, nothing. The Charger could have gotten off at a number of places, but I'll keep looking," Michelle said.

"I need to call the police and tell them about this," Emma said as she picked up her phone but then stopped as she remembered how Michelle got the images. "Oh, I can't do that," she said.

"Hey, if it helps the cops get off their asses and get a bead on where Shane went then fuck it, tell them, I don't give a shit if they want to charge me for hacking," Michelle said and Emma noted that Ben's girlfriend actually seemed pleased with herself when she made the remark. These two really are a good match, Emma thought.

"Listen, I don't think that will be necessary because I have an idea," Emma said. "I'll get Jason to call the officer in charge and tell him he got the images anonymously from someone who saw our Facebook and Instagram postings looking for information about Shane and wanted to help. Jason won't have any idea how the tipster got the screenshots."

Emma dialed Jason's number and even though it was almost 4 am, Jason had told her repeatedly that she was to call him at any time, day or night if she needed anything. She knew Jason was being sincere when he said it because Shane had solved several important cases for the lawyer and they had become close friends.

Emma was surprised when Jason answered on the second ring and said, "Emma, hi, how're you holding up? Is there any news?"

"I'm sorry for calling so early," Emma responded.

"I was up anyway," Jason said. "It's tough sleeping when you're worried about Shane, so I just gave up and I've been sitting at the kitchen table making notes on anything I can think of that may have put Shane in harm's way."

"I know what you're saying about sleep, that's for sure," Emma said. "I'm calling because Ben's girlfriend has come up with something I need to get to the police. I can't do it because of how it was obtained."

Emma told Jason about the images of the Charger they found and he readily agreed to get it to Sergeant Lucas, the Brantford officer in charge of Shane's case, using Emma's idea to explain where they came from. Jason was pleased about the lead because, like Emma, he knew that as each hour went by and there was no contact from someone who kidnapped Shane, if that's what happened to him, the active search for his friend would wind down and it would be assumed Shane was dead.

After telling Emma he would make the call, Jason said that he believed that if Shane's disappearance was not connected to Lan's situation and the Vietnamese-Canadian gang leader she was to testify against, then it had to be somehow connected to the last big case he worked on; the murder of Paige Madison and the Gavin Benson trial.

"If this isn't a case of Shane working on something dangerous I didn't know about, or perhaps he was in the wrong place at the wrong time, his involvement in the Benson trial is the only thing that makes sense," Jason said. "As you know, the details about what was done to Paige and the subsequent trial caused a sensation in the city and there was a lot of heated emotional reaction, much of it directed at Gavin Benson."

"But if this is about Benson, why now and why Shane?" Emma wondered. "I realize Shane was the investigator for the defence, but if someone wanted revenge, and I apologize for saying this, but why not go after you, Benson's lawyer? You were the one at the public trial trying to get Benson off on the murder charge. But he was found guilty, so if it's revenge because you failed, then it would have to be either a member of Benson's family or some sick individual who followed the case and was convinced Benson was innocent."

"I think there's a connection between Benson's suicide in jail this week and what's happened to Shane," Jason said. "And I'm going to continue to push that theory when I talk to Sergeant Lucas. They need to check on the movements over the past two days of the major players in the case. I'm going to get Chioma to do the same thing, but specifically Benson's wife Alison, his son Josh and his daughter Melissa and her husband Jake."

There was a moment of silence and then Emma said softly, "I'm desperately trying to keep it together, Jason, but I don't know for how much longer before I break down emotionally and become useless to everyone, and I can't do that to Lan because she needs me. In my heart, I'm hoping that someone has kidnapped Shane for a reason we don't know yet, and he hasn't been harmed. But my head tells me that since no one has been in contact something bad has happened, that Shane is dead."

There was more silence, but Jason didn't say anything because he knew Emma was trying to compose herself. After a moment, he said, "Emma, you're one of the strongest and most emotionally-centered people I know, so I know you'll get through this and we'll find Shane."

"I'm trying," Emma responded and then said in a strong voice, "So you'll get Chioma to look into the Benson family? What can I do to help? Ben and Michelle are here working hard, but I need to be doing something to help find Shane, I need to stay busy."

"There is one thing I've been thinking about," Jason said, "But it's a long shot and I don't want to say anything to the police because it might cause some unnecessary harm to the individual."

Jason then explained that during the course of the trial, the number of people watching the proceedings from the visitor's gallery fluctuated widely, which is normal as people lose interest or don't want to take any more time off work. There are, of course, the normal courtroom addicts, people who seem to have nothing better to do with their lives than watch trials, even if it's small claims court.

Paige's parents were there every day, Benson's daughter, Melissa, attended frequently, but she had a young child at home. Benson's son, Josh, wearing his Canadian Forces dress uniform, attended every day for the first week, but then had to return to duty.

"During the early days of the trial, some of Paige's friends attended sporadically, but never stayed long," Jason told Emma. "But there was one young man who sat through every minute of the trial. It didn't appear that he was a friend of Paige's because he never sat with the others, always by himself. He was not one of the regulars because I knew most of them."

"You think he's somehow connected to either the Bensons or Paige?" Emma asked.

"I don't know, he didn't take notes so I assume he wasn't a journalist covering the trial or someone maybe looking to write a book about a sensational murder," Jason said. "I don't know, there was just something about him that caught my attention."

Shane had told Emma that Jason was very talented at reading people and it was one of the reasons he was one of the top defence lawyers in Ontario. Shane had said that he had learned to trust Jason's instincts.

"So you don't know who this guy is?" Emma asked

"No, I never found out," Jason replied. "Out of curiosity I asked some of the regulars, but no one knew who he was and some called him kinda creepy. At one point I was thinking about asking Shane to check him out, but then I just moved on and put him down as a courtroom junkie I wasn't familiar with."

"And now you're thinking about him again?" Emma asked.

"I have been sitting here, unable to sleep, going over my notes and thinking about the case. I'm hoping the reason for this guy's presence is not something I missed, Jason replied. "Maybe he's Paige's actual murderer, attending the trial to get a sick thrill out of someone else being found responsible. Or maybe he's Paige's killer and angry that the wrong man was found guilty, took Shane, blaming him for not doing a better investigation. Maybe he wanted to get caught so he would be in the limelight at a trial. That's happened before. Or maybe he's not involved at all, but I need to know for sure."

"What can you tell me about him?" Emma asked and grabbed a pen and notepad that she had started keeping nearby all the time.

Jason said he only saw the young man from the waist up, but he had narrow shoulders, suggesting he had a slight build and appeared to be around the same age as Paige Madison. What stood out was his short, curly, bright red hair and very freckled face.

Jason knew there was no one Paige worked with who fit that description and he wondered if he was someone she went to school with.

"I would call Paige's friend, Ariel Durst, and ask her about him, but I'm sure she doesn't want to hear from me after the grilling I gave her at the trial," Jason said.

"No problem, I can do that, but I think I'll try and find out who he is first," Emma said.

"Okay, let me know," Jason said and then added, "Emma, stay positive about Shane. We're going to find him, alive."

Chapter Twelve - Present

Shane awoke with a slight headache, a very dry mouth and dull, throbbing pain in his damaged left knee, its usual reminder that it was there.

With the light in the room where he was being held always on and no watch, he had no idea what time it was or how long he had slept; it could have been five hours or maybe just one hour, he had no idea. He assumed it was night when he went to sleep because Josh had opened the trap door and pushed through a pillow, a thin gray blanket and a camping mattress, the kind you could roll up tight to carry on the top of a backpack and it self-inflated, although only to about three inches wide.

After depositing the stuff into the room, Josh had simply said, "Get some sleep," and then reached in to pull the trap closed. Shane, who was sitting on the floor reading through the Benson trial transcript for the third time, jumped to his feet and pleaded, "Josh, wait! Please talk to me! I have questions and things to tell you." Shane was hoping that if Josh thought he had found something that might help exonerate his father, then he wouldn't ignore him and simply close the opening.

"What have you found?" Josh asked.

Shane noted that his abductor's complexion looked waxen and he had dark circles under his bloodshot eyes, leading Shane to believe that, like him, Josh was sleep deprived, likely from spending hours watching the monitors from the cameras in the room.

Shane ignored Josh's question and said, "Josh, let's be honest here. I think you know full well that forcing me to read through the transcript of your father's trial is not going to lead me to tell you what you want to hear. This is your idea of revenge, pure and simple, and to somehow make yourself feel like you did something for your father. But what I don't understand is why it's me you kidnapped. Why didn't you grab Evan Gregory, the Prosecutor? He's the man who convinced the jury to convict your father. Or why isn't Jason Burke, your father's attorney, in this room instead of me?"

"No matter what you believe, I brought you here because you're intimately familiar with my father's case and you're supposed to be this hot shit detective who has, in the past, proven the police were wrong when they thought they had a case solved," Josh answered.

"But when I did that, I didn't do it from a locked room!" Shane responded. "I was free to question people and do research. What's the end game here, Josh? When I come up empty, which is what's going to happen, are you going to kill me?"

This time it was Josh who ignored a question and instead asked one of his own, "You said you had something to tell me. What did you find?"

Shane wasn't sure how to answer. He had said he had something only as a way to get Josh to talk to him in a desperate effort to try and convince Gavin Benson's son to give himself up. Shane did, in fact, read testimony in the trial transcript that had him wondering about an alternative theory of who killed Paige. But it was only a small seed of an idea and he wasn't even sure himself if it would lead anywhere, so he wasn't prepared to share it with Josh.

"I wanted to tell you that I do have some ideas that might, and I strongly emphasize might, help clear your father's name," Shane said. "But I can't go any further sitting in here, you have to let me go and investigate."

"That's not happening yet because I don't trust you," Josh said. "I don't trust anyone who was involved in framing my father for murder. But I'm prepared in case you came up with something."

Josh disappeared from the opening of the door, leaving Shane frustrated that he was at the mercy of a man who must have had some kind of mental breakdown because of his father's suicide and was unable to see the absurdity of what he was doing. There has to be a way out of this, Shane thought.

When Josh returned he had a cloth bag with something flat in it that was attached to a very thin piece of rope which he used to lower the bag from the hole in the door to the floor.

"Pick up the bag and get what's inside," Josh ordered Shane, who reached inside and pulled out a tablet.

"You probably don't know, but it's late at night, so you need to get some more sleep," Josh said. "Tomorrow morning when that tablet shows 9 am, you'll be able to open the email program where there's only one address that will work, the one for Chioma Abiola, who is listed on the Burke and Associates website as your Researcher. You can ask her to send you any files you need or get her to do any interviews you need, or she can get your partner Emma to do them. I read she's been involved in some of your cases."

"Josh, as soon as they know that I'm alive and being held against my will, there will be a full-court press to find the location of this tablet," Shane said.

"They can try but I can guarantee they'll never do it," Josh said. "The IP address constantly changes, bouncing around between servers all over the world. It will take them months just to figure out a pattern and by then it will have changed anyway. Plus, in your first email, you will tell them that if they try to introduce a worm, virus or search algorithm in their return emails or files, I will know and I won't hesitate to shoot you in the head. I will be monitoring every keystroke you make and when you hit send, it won't go until I agree. If you try to hide clues about who's holding you or where you are, although I doubt you have a clue about your location, I will shoot you."

"Josh, I'm begging you to think about what you're doing here!" Shane pleaded. "Even if I don't provide any information in the first email, it won't take long before the police figure out who kidnapped me. In fact, I suspect they probably already know it's you if they've been checking on the whereabouts of people connected to my recent cases. And if they haven't figured it out yet, I can guarantee that either Emma has or my friend, Ben Chen, who is brilliant with computers and can be like a dog with a bone."

"I don't care, I assumed they would find out it was me," Josh said without a trace of concern in his voice. "I'm giving you a chance to save your own life by correcting the mistake made by the police, you and your lawyer boss when you didn't find out who really killed Paige and caused my father to take his own life."

"I still don't get it, Josh," Shane said. "I completely understand that you're angry about what happened to your father and that you're convinced he didn't kill Paige, but you still haven't explained why you're willing to throw your own life away in a misguided attempt to force someone to tell you what you want to hear."

Josh didn't say anything and just looked at Shane with a neutral expression on his face. Shane knew that what he was going to say next could backfire and Josh would get so angry that he would kill him immediately. But if Josh said it was true and it was finally out in the open, maybe Shane could convince him to give himself up.

"Josh," Shane said. "Are you doing this because you know for a fact your father was innocent? You found out somehow that your father was having an affair with a woman young enough to be your sister and you blamed Paige for starting it. Angry that she's going to break up your family, you assault and kill her, and then dump her body in a field, hoping police will believe that she was the random victim of a sexual predator."

"But then your father is arrested and charged with Paige's murder," Shane continued, "But you weren't worried because your father had one of the best defence lawyers in Ontario with a perfect track record of having his clients found innocent. But that didn't work, your father was found guilty and then committed suicide. You decide that if you come forward and confess to the killing, the police won't believe you, saying that it's a misguided effort, because of your anger and grief, to clear your father's name. So then you decide to do something, namely kidnap me, to try and force someone to prove it was you who murdered Paige."

"You're wrong, I didn't kill Paige," Josh said. "I don't care what happens to me because I'm dying."

Chapter Thirteen - The Trial

Like her late friend, Paige Madison, Ariel Durst was a beautiful young woman, but unlike Paige, who had been a blonde with blue eyes and fair skin, Ariel had long dark hair, brown eyes and an olive complexion, thanks to the Italian heritage on her mother's side of the family.

Ariel was also a poised, well spoken and credible witness for the Crown in Gavin Benson's murder trial. She had dressed conservatively for her time on the witness chair; a light brown jacket and skirt combo, an off-white blouse and flat shoes. Her makeup looked perfectly applied, suggesting she knew what she was doing when it came to highlighting her natural good looks, and she had her hair pulled back and tied in a ponytail.

Jason knew that Ariel's testimony was critical to the Prosecutor if he wanted to prove that Benson had a strong motive to kill Paige and she didn't disappoint in that regard. Evan Gregory skillfully led her through the history of her friendship with Paige and the various discussions the two young women had about their romantic relationships.

Gregory's questioning eventually reached the critical part of Ariel's testimony; what Paige told her about her affair with Gavin Benson, including that she was pregnant and planned to tell Gavin about it the day she was murdered. Ariel testified that Paige told her that if

Gavin didn't agree to leave his wife right away so they could be together, then she would tell Alison Benson about their relationship. Ariel claimed that Paige was worried about how Gavin would react, especially if she had to threaten to tell his wife about what was going on if he didn't seek a divorce.

"Did you get the impression that Paige was worried the defendant would react physically against her for getting pregnant and threatening to tell his wife," Gregory asked.

"Objection," Jason said as he stood up. "Your Honour, Ms. Durst can testify to what Ms. Madison said to her, but can't know how she felt."

"I agree," Judge Garnet ruled.

Jason was surprised Garnet didn't say, 'I tend to agree', this time.

"Mr. Gregory, please keep your questions to the witness specifically about statements made by Ms. Madison," Garnet said.

Gregory nodded his head at the Judge as a sign of respect for the ruling and then returned his attention to Ariel and asked, "Leaving aside your personal impression of how Paige felt, did she specifically say anything to you about how she was feeling about what was going on with the defendant?"

"She said she was positive that Gavin loved her, but was concerned that he seemed to be dragging his feet about telling his wife about them and asking her for a divorce," Ariel said. "I told her that was already not a good sign and now she was planning to tell him she was pregnant. She said Gavin had a quick temper and she hoped he didn't react badly. I think she was scared."

"Your Honour," Jason started but Judge Garnet held up his hand to keep him from continuing, turned toward Ariel and said, "Ms. Durst, you must only say what Ms. Madison actually told you."

"Yes, your Honour," Ariel responded.

"But just to confirm, Paige told you she hoped the defendant, Gavin Benson, didn't react badly," Gregory said.

"Yes she did," Paige said firmly.

It was damning testimony and combined with what Benson's business partner told the trial and Gavin's demonstration of a quick temper with his angry outburst in the courtroom, the Prosecutor had given the jury good reasons to believe Gavin had a strong motive to murder Paige.

Jason had argued strenuously during voir dire, the trial within a trial when no jury is present, that most of Ariel's testimony about what Paige told her was hearsay and therefore inadmissible. He reminded Judge Garnet that in her statement to police, Ariel said she was angry at Paige for getting involved with a man old enough to be her father and during the preliminary hearing testified that even though she didn't know him, she hated Benson for what she believed he had done to her friend. Jason argued that Ariel had a clear motive to fabricate what Paige told her the day she was murdered and that made her testimony hearsay and inadmissible during the trial.

In his rebuttal, Crown Prosecutor Gregory said that Ariel's testimony clearly fell under the Ante Mortem Exception, which holds that in a murder trial, the court will allow a witness to testify as to statements made by the victim about the accused before he or she died.

In the 1990 case, R. v. Khan, the Supreme Court of Canada set out a new method for determining whether hearsay statements should be admitted for trial. It involved a two-step approach, the first being the court determining whether it was necessary to use the out of court statement or if there was another way to admit the evidence. At the second step of the Khan test, the court must determine whether the hearsay evidence is reliable. In the 2006 case R. v. Khelowan, the Supreme Court suggested that judges could look at all factors, including the substance of the testimony and the surrounding evidence to determine whether a statement is reliable and can be admitted during the trial as an exception to the rule against hearsay.

As Jason had expected, it didn't take long for Judge Garnet to rule that Ariel Durst's testimony about what Paige told her before she was murdered was an exception to the hearsay rules and would be allowed. He said it would be up to the jury to decide the veracity of Ariel's testimony after she had been questioned by the prosecution and cross-examined by the defence. While Jason anticipated the ruling, he wanted his challenge on the record in the event that Gavin was found guilty. If, during his cross examination of Ariel, he was able to get her to testify to a significant bias against Benson both before and after Paige's death, it would be additional grounds for an appeal of his conviction.

After Gregory said he had completed his questioning of Ariel, Judge Garnet called the lunch recess and told Jason he could begin his cross-examination in the afternoon session.

When the trial resumed and Ariel was back on the witness chair, Jason did a last minute shuffling of his notes on the table in front of him and mentally confirmed his strategy. While he intended to be aggressive in his questioning of Ariel to try and counter some of her damaging testimony, he had to be careful not to alienate the jury. He recognized that during her testimony earlier in the day, Ariel came across as a nice, likeable young woman who cared deeply about her murdered friend, so he didn't want the jury to think he was trying to bully her. It was going to be a very fine line.

Jason got up from his chair and walked around to stand just in front of the defence table. He smiled and said, "Good afternoon, Ariel. Your friendship with Paige was very important to you."

"Yes, it was," Ariel responded. "We had been close friends for a long time and up until the time she got involved with Gavin, we never argued or spoke harshly to each other."

"About that," Jason said and then asked, "Why weren't you at least a little bit happy and supportive of your best friend who had found love and was thrilled about having a child with him?"

"Because I thought she was being naive about her relationship with a man old enough to be her father," Ariel answered. "I couldn't understand how she believed the guy actually loved her."

"So you knew what was best for Paige?" Jason asked before Ariel could go any further.

"No, I'm not saying that," Ariel answered defensively. "I was just trying to be the voice of reason, to point out the reality of her situation."

"Prior to you becoming aware that Paige was involved with my client, did she ever express an interest in older men as opposed to men her own age?" Jason asked.

"Yes," Ariel answered. "Often when we were out at a club with friends, she would show no interest in dancing or hanging with the guys who approached her."

"Paige was a beautiful woman, so I imagine there were lots of them," Jason interrupted.

"Oh, for sure, Paige was pretty popular with the guys. It was always like that, even when we were in school," Ariel said.

"Did she ever date guys her own age?" Jason asked.

"Oh, sure, sometimes, but there was never anything serious," Ariel answered. "She was always telling me how she wanted a more mature relationship, free of all the drama people our age seemed to relish in."

"Before she got involved in a serious relationship with my client, Mr. Benson, did Paige do what she said she wanted to do, date older men?" Jason asked.

"Not as far as I know, no," Ariel said. "It was just something she talked about."

"Is it possible Paige was involved with other older men before my client and chose not to tell you?" Jason asked and before Ariel could answer, he added, "After all, she was involved with my client for quite some time before she decided to tell you in confidence that she was in a serious relationship and was pregnant."

"Well, that might be true, but as I said, I was not aware of any previous relationships," Ariel said, a defensive tone becoming apparent.

"But there could have been, right?" Jason pushed.

"Yes, I suppose," Ariel said.

"And so it's possible that Paige was involved with other older men before my client, chose not to tell you, and maybe one of those relationships ended badly, leaving Paige's former lover, maybe a married man, angry and revengeful," Jason stated.

"Your Honour," Gregory said as he stood up, "My colleague is not asking a question of this witness but speculating about facts that are not before this court."

"Mr. Burke, if you want to show that Ms. Madison had previous relationships, then you can do that when you present your defence," Judge Garnet ruled. "Please move on."

"Yes, your Honour," Jason responded and then said to Ariel, "My client's business partner, Ethan Holdaway, testified that Paige was ambitious, a flirt who used her good looks to get ahead at work. Would you agree with that description of your friend?"

Gregory was quickly on his feet again and said, "Your Honour, Mr. Burke seems intent on disparaging the victim in this case and that should not be allowed."

"Your Honour, the Prosecutor has made a big deal about the close relationship between Ms. Durst and Ms. Madison, and that they didn't keep secrets from each other," Jason responded. "Mr. Gregory has purposely done this through this witness's testimony in order to try and lend credibility to what Ms. Durst claims the victim told her the day before Paige was murdered. I should be allowed to challenge that."

"I will allow your questions in this regard," Judge Garnet ruled and then quickly added in a stern voice, "But Mr. Burke, the victim is not on trial here, so be very careful how you frame your questions or I will shut you down."

"I understand, Your Honour," Jason said.

"Make sure you do, Mr. Burke," Garnet said firmly.

Jason turned to face Ariel again and said. "So, Ariel, back to my question. Did you know Paige to be ambitious and to use her good looks and charm on men in order to achieve her ambitions, as claimed by my client's business partner?"

"Not at all," Ariel answered firmly. "Paige was very confident about achieving her goals in life. However, as I said, anytime we were together around guys our own age she could be standoffish. But I have no idea how she acted at work."

"She never talked to you about what went on at her job? Never shared any gossip? Maybe said she had the men wrapped around her finger?" Jason asked.

Jason noted and he hoped the jury also noticed that the poised and confident manner that Ariel had demonstrated during her questioning by the Prosecutor had disappeared. She appeared nervous and tense, sat forward on her chair and no longer had her legs crossed in a casual manner.

"The Paige I knew my whole life wasn't like that!" Paige exclaimed.

"But it appears that maybe you didn't know Paige as well as you said you did," Jason said and before Paige could respond, he asked, "You testified that you never met my client, is that correct?"

Paige, still trying to process what happened during Jason's previous questions, hesitated before confirming that she had never met Mr. Benson.

"And you testified that you got upset with Paige when she told you she had been having an affair with Mr. Benson and that she was pregnant. Correct?" Jason asked.

"That's correct, I did," Ariel answered.

"And after Paige told you and you got upset with her, did you form a personal opinion of Mr. Benson, even though you never met him?" Jason asked.

"Well, I did resent him because I thought he had taken advantage of Paige and was stringing her along with his claims he cared for her just so he could have sex with a much younger woman," Ariel answered.

"You resented him, but were you also angry at him? Did you start to hate him?" Jason asked.

"Not hate, I didn't hate him, but yes, I was angry," Ariel said.

"And what about now?" Jason asked as he turned from Ariel in the witness chair to draw her attention to Gavin, who was sitting stoically at the defence table. "Do you hate him now? Enough that you've embellished what Paige actually told you the day before she was killed because, as we've established, you really didn't know Paige that well and she kept secrets from you?"

"No, that's not true!" Ariel said in a loud voice.

"Your Honour, Mr. Burke, who has already been badgering this witness, is now accusing her of perjury with no foundation for doing it," Gregory protested.

Jason, who was facing Ariel in the witness box, turned to where Gregory was standing at his table and said, "I think I've established a very good foundation for asking Ms. Durst if she's embellished what the victim told her."

"Please direct your comments to me, Mr. Burke," Judge Garnet admonished.

"I apologize, your Honour," Jason said as he turned and looked at Garnet.

"I would tend to agree with Mr. Gregory that your foundation for questioning this witness about the veracity of what she says she was told is thin," Garnet said to Jason.

Jason didn't consider Garnet's latest use of 'tend to agree' as an actual ruling but decided he had pushed Ariel as far as he should, so he said, "I understand, your Honour, but I'm finished questioning Ms. Durst anyway."

"Very well, Mr. Burke," Garnet said and then asked the Prosecutor, "Any redirect Mr. Gregory?"

"A brief one, your Honour," Gregory said and after waiting for Jason to return to the defence table and sit down, he said, "Ariel, I appreciate the bravery you've shown today answering what must be painful questions about the death of your best friend. Is anything my colleague has been trying to suggest true? In your statement to the police and in your testimony today, did you add anything or change anything that Paige said to you?"

"Absolutely not," Ariel answered with conviction.

"That's all I have for redirect, your Honour," Gregory told the Judge. As Ariel walked from the witness chair to the visitor benches to sit with some friends who had attended to support her, Jason wondered just how much success he had in undermining her credibility with the jury.

Gavin, who had shown no emotion during Ariel's testimony, muttered softly to Jason, "Nice try."

Chapter Fourteen - Present

It didn't take long for Emma to identify the red-headed young man who attended the Benson trial every day.

After talking to Jason on the phone, Emma wanted to start doing some research right away, but realized she should at least try and get some sleep or she would be too exhausted to function properly. She didn't bother undressing, laid on top of the covers on her bed, and closed her eyes, not expecting anything to happen. However, the next thing she knew she was opening her eyes and the bedside clock said it was 7 am. A sense of purpose had finally allowed her mind to be calm enough so she could sleep.

After going to the bathroom and using the toilet, Emma washed her face, brushed her teeth and then went to the kitchen where Lan was sitting at the table eating a bowl of cereal and watching a video on the tablet sitting on its stand in front of her.

"Good morning, Emma. Did you get some sleep? I was worried about you," Lan said, looking up from her tablet.

"A little bit, and good morning to you too," Emma said with a smile. "I don't want you to worry about me, Lan, I'm fine."

Ben and Michelle's laptops were sitting closed on the table and Emma was glad the two had finally decided to go to their hotel and get some sleep. At first, Emma thought their arrival at her house would be a disruption she didn't need, but now she was glad they were here and they had already found some important information about Shane's possible whereabouts.

After Lan finished her breakfast, she went to get washed and dressed for school, and then to spend some time in her room before it was time for Emma to walk her out to the street to catch her bus. Emma made coffee, trying to not think about how much she had consumed over the past twenty four hours, and took a mug to the table where her laptop also sat.

Jason had provided her with background information on Paige Madison which included the fact that she attended secondary school at Brantford Collegiate, the same school Emma had graduated from, albeit quite a few years earlier than Paige, the passage of such a long time was something Emma didn't want to think about.

Emma maintained a membership with the BCI alumni group and so had access to its website, which contained electronic copies of the historic school's yearbooks, dating back decades. Paige was twenty two years old when she was killed, so Emma thought she likely graduated at the end of the 2015 school year and that was the yearbook Emma selected on the website. The book was in pdf format and Emma quickly scrolled to the photographs of the graduating students where she found both Paige Madison and her friend Ariel Durst. The note under Paige's picture said she was a member of the volleyball and track and field teams and was 'bound to rule an office one day'. Ariel was also involved in track and field as well as gymnastics and the note under her photo said she was 'BCI's official boy magnet'. Emma wasn't surprised by Ariel's yearbook tag because she was a beautiful girl, as was Paige.

Emma was glad the photographs of the graduates were in colour, which was not the case back when she was in school, because she could look specifically for students with red hair and not just guys with curly hair if the photos were in black and white.

Emma found ten graduating males with red hair, but only one had both short, curly hair and a heavily freckled face. His name was Logan Stewart and, like Paige and Ariel, he was a member of the track and field team. No other interests were listed under his name and he was called the 'President of the P Fan Club'. If this was the young man she was looking for, Emma wondered if the 'P' stood for Paige and if it did, that would explain why he attended every minute of the murder trial. Was Logan Stewart infatuated with Paige and wanted to see the man accused of her murder on trial and found guilty? Or maybe, as Jason suggested, he was the person who actually killed Paige and wanted to watch someone else go to jail for it.

But, at this point, the only thing that mattered to Emma was whether or not this Logan had something to do with Shane's disappearance. Shane was meticulous when it came to his investigations and she knew he was successful because he never accepted everything he was told as a fact. "There's seldom black and white with the people I talk to during an investigation, especially if it involves murder," Shane would say and often remarked that he was amazed by how many great liars there were.

During dinners at home, both before and during the trial, Shane would often express his frustration at being unable to uncover anything that might help Jason prove definitively that Gavin Benson was innocent.

"I know Jason believes his client, but I'm coming up with nothing," Shane complained one night. "I'm convinced I'm missing something and I can't figure out what it is."

"Is there anything I can do to help?" Emma had asked and then Lan added, "I'll help too, Shane, but I know you got this."

The comment brought a smile to Shane's face and he said, "Thanks, Lan, you've restored my confidence."

"No problem," Lan said and went back to eating her dinner.

Emma wondered if Shane didn't give up on the case after the trial ended and Benson was found guilty. She wouldn't be surprised at all if Shane kept digging on his own time, looking for an elusive fact he might have missed. Did Shane also research the trial watcher, find Logan Stewart as she did, and then on the day he disappeared decide to go and talk to Stewart? Is it possible that when Shane started asking probing questions, Stewart believed he was about to be exposed as Paige's real killer, panicked, and took Shane captive? Emma was also aware that Stewart, if he had already committed one murder, probably wouldn't hesitate to kill Shane. But she put that thought aside, she had to, or she would fall apart emotionally.

After Emma saw Lan safely onto her bus, she showered, put on some fresh jeans and a light top, and applied some makeup to cover up the dark circles under her eyes. By the time she returned to the kitchen, Ben and Michelle were there, both intensely working on their laptops. Emma had given Ben a house key knowing he would be coming and going at odd hours.

"I'm glad you two finally went and got some sleep," Emma said as she poured herself another mug of coffee.

Michelle, who Emma noted had somehow managed to look rested and fresh, stopped what she was doing on her laptop, and said excitingly, "Ben's got something!"

Ben also stopped what he was doing, smiled at Emma, and said, "Fucking right I do."

Emma pulled a chair around and sat down beside him so she could see the screen on his laptop and asked, "What did you find?"

Ben replied, "While Michelle continued to search saved footage from whatever cameras she could connect to for further images of Shane's Charger and where it might have gone, I've been doing a deep fucking dive into the social media accounts of the main people connected to Paige Matheson and Gavin Benson."

Ben worked some keys on his laptop and brought up a split screen; on the left was the homepage for Josh Benson's Facebook account and on the right was the same for his Instagram. Ben explained that dating back to when Gavin Benson was first arrested for murder, Josh posted something to both sites on a daily basis, as well as a comment on X, which used to be Twitter, declaring his father's innocence and ranting about how the police have got it wrong and how his father was being railroaded by the justice system.

Ben brought up some examples on his laptop and said to Emma, "As you can see, he posted a lot of pictures of his father with his mother and with him and his sister, all with the same captions, either 'Not A Killer' or 'Innocent'. He was totally fucking obsessed with his father's case. No personal posts."

Ben brought up two more images and said, "Every time there was a newspaper article, TV news story or online post about his father's case or damning testimony during the trial, Josh would re-post it and put the word 'Wrong' or 'False' in big bold fucking letters under it. And he had some rather nasty fucking exchanges with anyone who disagreed with his comments on his posts to X or called his father a killer. I'm surprised X didn't cut him off."

"He was obviously very close to his father and passionate about his innocence," Emma said and then asked, "What about his sister, Melissa, same thing?"

"Not nearly as much," Ben replied. "At first, yes, she and many of her Facebook friends expressed their support for her father and his innocence, but once more details about the case against him came out and the testimony at the trial started, she took down all of the pictures of her father and made no further posts about him as if he no longer fucking existed."

"So, are you thinking that Josh's passion for his father's innocence has led to him kidnapping Shane? Is he doing it because of his father's conviction and eventual suicide?" Emma asked.

"Yes! And here's fucking why," Ben said excitedly. "What I'm showing you is Josh's social media accounts that I had to recover because he had taken everything down the day his father was found guilty. When people cancel their Facebook pages and Instagram accounts, they think that's the fucking end of it, but nothing is gone forever on the internet if you know how to retrieve it."

"Okay, but just to play Devil's Advocate, maybe after his father's conviction, Josh felt his social media proclamations about his father's innocence were too painful to deal with anymore, so he got rid of them," Emma said.

"But given the aggressive nature of his daily posts claiming his father's innocence, I can't see Josh just giving up and shutting it all down," Michelle said as she turned from her laptop to join the discussion. "Unless he suddenly developed another fucking obsession, like getting revenge on the people who failed to keep his father out of jail."

"Okay, assuming that's true," Emma said. "I'll say the same thing I told Jason; why Shane and not him? Jason was his father's lawyer, so why wouldn't Josh go after him? Or why not Evan Gregory, the Crown Prosecutor, who convinced the jury his father was guilty?"

"Who knows how an obsessed mind works?" Michelle responded. "Maybe Shane was the easiest target? Maybe Josh thought Shane didn't work hard enough to find out who really killed Paige. Josh would have met Shane, maybe he simply didn't like him."

"Either way, we need to find out where Josh is right now," Emma said. "It's assumed that he's back at Borden, but that needs to be confirmed. Jason said that Chioma was tracking the recent movements of the key people involved in the trial, including Josh, so I'm going to call her this morning to see what she's got. This is important stuff you've found. Thank you."

"There's something else I want to show you," Ben said and then after working the keyboard on his laptop brought up a Facebook page called 'Remembering Paige', which featured a large photograph of Paige Madison in the banner. Ben explained that it was a Facebook Group set up by friends of Paige shortly after she was killed and was moderated by an Emily Watson. Ben scrolled through the site to show Emma the various posts to the site; heartfelt tributes and dozens of pictures of Paige at various ages, some by herself and many with friends.

"She was obviously very popular," Emma commented. "Her murder was a terrible tragedy."

"This site was up for only about a month after Paige's death," Ben said. "It was open to the public, so you didn't have to join the Group to post something, and the moderator allowed anonymous posts, which I think is always a fucking mistake, and is probably why this Emily Watson took it down. In particular, likely because of this fucking guy, or who I assume was a guy."

Ben isolated a long series of anonymous posts to the site from someone who used the tag, 'Always Paige' and a blank profile picture. The posts contained flowery tributes to Paige, love poems and pictures, many of which, Ben pointed out, appeared to have been taken without Paige being aware she was being photographed because she's never looking at the camera. The shots included Paige standing at a school locker, getting into her car, walking out the front door of a house, and opening a door to enter what appears to be a business, probably where she worked.

"Was this guy a stalker?" Emma asked.

"You sure get that fucking impression," Ben said.

"If you post anonymously to a Facebook Group, doesn't the administrator or the moderator of the site still get to see your name and profile picture?" Emma asked.

It was Michelle who answered. "And it's available to the people at Facebook as well," she said. "But it's pretty easy to set up an anonymous Facebook account and profile. You sign up using what's called a 'burner email address' which can't be connected to you, a random phone number using a real area code, a false name, made-up personal information and some generic photo you found on the internet."

"But this guy, whoever he was, knew Paige because of the pictures he posted," Emma said.

"There's more," Ben said as he pulled up more posts on the site from 'Always Paige.' Emma looked at the screen on the laptop and saw a series of individual posts that were text only. The comments were always in bold capital letters and included: 'We all know who killed our Paige!', 'We need capital punishment for people like Gavin Benson!', and 'Let's support our Paige by watching her killer's trial and cheering when he's found guilty!'.

Emma noted that after each of the rants, either Emily Watson or Ariel Durst asked the writer not to make such posts because that was not the purpose of the Facebook Page, it was for remembering Paige. That sparked a series of comments from people who either agreed with Emily and Ariel or supported the things being posted by 'Always Paige'.

"As you can see, Emily basically lost control of the Group," Ben said. "I think she felt it was too late to make the Group private, so she just shut the fucking thing down."

"So there's no way to find out who this 'Always Paige' is?" Emma asked.

"Not the real person," Ben answered and brought up a new screen on his laptop. "After I recovered the Facebook Group, it didn't take me long to hack the moderator page and get the info for the obsessed asshole 'Always Paige', but it's a safe bet it's all fake."

Emma looked briefly at the page Ben brought up on the screen. The profile picture was a head shot of what looked like a middle-aged man wearing dark horn-rimmed glasses who said his location was Brantford. The name was Ryan Gosling.

"You know, as in Ryan Gosling, the actor," Michelle said.

"Real clever," Emma remarked facetiously and then said, "I wonder if there's a chance this Paige admirer is the same guy I'm looking into."

Emma held up her phone and showed Ben and Michelle the yearbook picture of Logan Stewart that she had grabbed online and explained she believed this was a young man Jason told her had attended the entire Benson trial. Emma said she had texted the picture to Jason and was waiting to hear back.

"You're thinking this is someone who was obsessed with Paige, maybe this fucking 'Always Paige' guy, and is involved in Shane's disappearance?" Ben asked.

Emma then shared her theory that after the Benson trial ended and he was found guilty, Shane didn't stop investigating Paige's murder and that led him to Logan Stewart, perhaps Paige's real killer.

"So when Shane confronts this Stewart, he takes Shane hostage," Michelle said, but Emma knew that was not what Michelle, or Ben, were actually thinking. They didn't want to upset her by saying Stewart may have killed Shane.

Before Emma could say anything further, her phone pinged. "It's Jason," she said and opened his text. "Jason says it's him, the guy observing the trial."

Ben and Michelle immediately turned to their laptops and began searching for Logan Stewart, but stopped when Emma said, "There's something else. Jason says that during her new round of research into everyone connected to the Benson case, Chioma found out that Benson's son, Josh, has received a medical discharge from the Canadian Forces."

Emma knew that Jason wouldn't ask Chioma how she got that information because he didn't want to know. Shane had told her many times that Chioma was an outstanding researcher with superior computer skills, which included the ability to get into restricted websites and databases where she legally shouldn't be. Both Shane and Jason knew better than to ask Chioma how she came up with some of her information because if she told them, then they would be a party to her illegal hacking. In reality, playing dumb about Chioma's sources probably wouldn't prevent legal issues for both men.

"Jason says, so far, Chioma has been unable to determine where Josh is currently, and whether or not he's returned to Brantford," Emma said as she continued to read Jason's text.

"So, what, you're thinking that if this fucker Josh Benson is out of the army, he could have grabbed Shane in revenge for not doing more to help his father who has now committed suicide?" Ben asked.

"It's another possibility, but I keep coming back to the question of why Shane?" Emma said. "Why not blame Jason, his father's lawyer, and kidnap him? Or the Crown Prosecutor?"

"Maybe it's like you suggested about this fucker Logan Stewart," Michelle said. "Maybe Shane was continuing his investigation into Paige's murder and found something that implicated Josh. And then, just like Chioma just did, he finds out Josh has been discharged from the army and is back in the city, so he goes to see him and starts asking questions. Josh thinks the jig is up, so he grabs Shane."

"I think we have two people to try and track down," Emma said and without a word, Ben and Michelle turned back to their laptops and started working the keyboards.

Emma wrote a return text to Jason thanking him for the information and asking him to thank Chioma for her efforts. She told Jason that Ben and Michelle were trying to collect information on Logan Stewart and that they had found some disturbing posts on a now-closed Facebook account dedicated to Paige that might be connected to Stewart. After sending the text, Emma poured herself more coffee and watched Shane's best friend and his girlfriend work the internet.

Ben always spoke his mind, and never in a socially or politically correct manner, but Emma always felt, and Shane agreed, that Ben kept a lot of his true feelings bottled up. She knew it was a safe bet that Shane's disappearance would be tearing Ben up inside and he would be desperate to find something, anything, that showed Shane was still alive. They had saved each other's lives on several occasions and a couple of years ago when Ben was accused of murdering his elderly neighbour, Shane proved he was innocent. Despite being complete opposites, there was an unbreakable bond between the two men.

Emma's thoughts were interrupted when Ben said, "Logan Stewart is a fucking ghost."

"What do you mean?" Emma asked.

"A Logan Stewart in Brantford has no presence on social media," Ben answered. "No Facebook, Instagram, X, TikTok or YouTube. Highly unlikely for someone in his age group unless he's a total fucking introvert."

"Maybe he's set up his accounts using a fake name and profile, just like the guy posting to Paige's memorial, who could be Logan," Emma said.

"I have no doubt that's exactly what he's done," Ben responded. "But if so, you have to wonder why. People use Facebook,

Instagram and other sites like Snapchat to communicate with friends and family, and to connect with people from around the world with similar interests. It's called social media for a fucking reason. Anyone who hides their internet presence behind an avatar and a false profile is doing it for nefarious reasons or is a voyeur."

"Shit, Ben, tell us how you really feel," Michelle said and then giggled, which Emma thought made her sound like a little girl, albeit one who looked like a Goth. Emma then realized that Michelle was more accurately like an emo kid, with her skinny jeans, thick black eyeliner, tight t-shirt with the name Paramore on it, a band she'd never heard of, studded belt and flat, straight, jet-black hair with long bangs. Emma was a classic rock fan, loved AC/DC, so didn't know much about emo music, other than it's a style of hardcore punk with very emotional lyrics.

Ben smiled at Michelle and didn't respond to her wisecrack, which surprised Emma, and then Michelle looked at the screen on her laptop and said, "There are nine L. Stewarts listed in Brantford, not surprising given how common the name is. I'll have to do some hacking into local databases to see if one has a first name Logan and then get the address."

"I think he probably lives in his parent's fucking basement," Ben commented.

"Listen, don't worry about any of that," Emma said. "I'm going to go and catch Paige's friend Ariel Durst before she goes to work and ask her about Logan. She should be able to tell me about him, maybe where he lives and works, and his connection with, or perhaps obsession with Paige."

"Just out of curiosity, are we going to be sharing any of this with the cops?" Michelle asked.

"I have to say that because of Shane's reputation, Brantford Police have been great right from the start trying to find him," Emma said. "And they pulled out all the stops trying to find the Charger in the early hours of his disappearance. But enough time has passed without communication from a kidnapper, so it's assumed there won't be one. It's a missing persons case now and Shane's picture and description have been distributed to all city officers and the OPP detachments in Southern Ontario. It's also been posted to the police services' public websites."

"So, at this point, they just wait until someone spots Shane," Michelle said hesitantly.

"It's okay, Michelle, you can say it. Or until his body is found," Emma said softly and try as she might, she couldn't stop some tears from trickling down her face.

"Fuck the police, they can all jam their badges where the sun doesn't shine!" Ben exclaimed. "We know that Shane is not dead and some motherfucker is holding him hostage and we are going to find him!"

"Thanks, Ben, for your confidence," Emma said. "I think we need to find Logan Stewart and Josh Benson because I believe one of them is involved."

Chapter Fifteen - The Trial

"The defence calls Doctor William Jacobs," Jason announced and stood at his table while a court officer left through the door at the back of the courtroom to get Jacobs who would be sitting on one of the benches in the hallway waiting to be called.

The Benson trial had adjourned for the day at mid-afternoon yesterday when the Prosecutor, Evan Gregory, told Judge Garnet the Crown had completed presenting its case to the jury. Jason had spent the rest of the day and well into the evening in his office going over his trial notes and his defence strategy, which was still a work in progress and he knew it shouldn't be. He still had some decisions to make and that was not normally how he handled a jury trial.

Well before the first day in court, based on the case laid out by the Crown at the preliminary hearing, Jason would know exactly what he was going to do when it came time for him to present his defence. He would have lined up both expert witnesses to refute any forensic evidence which could be questioned, and character witnesses in support of his client's innocence. And under no circumstance would he allow his client to testify in his own defence, because it would expose him or her to probing and often damaging questions from the prosecution.

Before the start of the trial, Jason suffered a legal setback, which he still couldn't believe happened, when the Crown Prosecutor managed to have expert testimony about the tire tracks found in the field near where Paige's body was discovered ruled admissible.

Jason had argued it would prejudice the jury if a forensic specialist was allowed to say the tracks were made from Goodyear tires found standard on Jeep Cherokees like the one driven by Gavin Benson. Jason submitted data showing there were hundreds of Cherokees registered in the Brantford area with Goodyear tires, not to mention the thousands of vehicles that had the same after-market tire. He also cited case law where the science of tire track evidence had been challenged as scientifically unreliable. He was unable to sway Judge Garnet who ruled the tire track evidence would be allowed.

One of the things that Jason didn't challenge because it was irrefutable was the expert testimony that the DNA from the semen in Paige's body and the fetus of her unborn child was a match to Gavin.

When it came right down to it, Jason knew the Crown's strongest argument that Gavin killed Paige was testimony from several witnesses that showed he had both motive and opportunity to commit the murder. This was the area where Jason had to concentrate his defence strategy, but there were a number of roadblocks. Gavin admitted he was with Paige and they had sex the morning she was killed but denies Paige told him she was pregnant and that she threatened to tell his wife if he didn't file for divorce right away so they could be together. But Ariel Durst testified that

Paige told her that was what she planned to do and despite Jason's best effort during cross-examination to question her credibility, he knew Ariel came across as honest and sincere.

Jason wanted the jury to hear that Gavin was a man who was not capable of hurting another human being, but finding character witnesses turned out to be a problem. Gavin was by no means a social person, a bit of a workaholic, and he told Jason he really didn't have any close friends, other than his partner Ethan Holdaway, but that was over since Holdaway testified against him. Gavin told Jason that most of the people he knew socially he met through his wife and when he was arrested and Alison filed for divorce, they all snubbed him.

Before the start and now, during the trial, Gavin kept insisting that he be allowed to testify, to tell his side of the story, that he loved Paige and he intended to leave his wife for her, and to refute any suggestion he would harm her. Jason kept explaining to Gavin why it's seldom a good idea for the defendant in a murder trial to testify, but Gavin claimed he had nothing to hide.

Jason had basically made up his mind that he really didn't have a lot of choice but to put Gavin on the stand and hope that if his testimony came across as truthful, it would raise reasonable doubt in the minds of the jurors. But Jason wanted to set the stage before putting Gavin on the stand. After he waived his right to confidentiality, Jason had spent several hours talking to Gavin's psychiatrist, William Jacobs, and was satisfied that if the doctor testified, what he had to say about his conversations with Gavin would help his defence.

Prosecutor Gregory tried to raise the same type of hearsay objections that Jason used prior to Ariel Durst's testimony, but after Jason submitted the psychiatrist's notes and tapes from his sessions with Gavin as evidence, Judge Garnet overruled any objections.

Jason began his questioning of Jacobs by asking him to outline his professional background, but the doctor wasn't far into his impressive educational resume when Gregory said the Crown had no problem with the psychiatrist's qualifications as an expert witness. Jason was pleased to see that Jacobs appeared calm and relaxed on the witness chair, his right leg over his left, hands on his lap but not clenched, and the jacket on his not too expensive looking suit unbuttoned. The doctor was dark complected with thinning, salt and pepper hair, medium build with a slight, middle-aged paunch showing above the belt of his pants, pointed nose, thin lips, and wearing stylish dark-rimmed glasses.

"Doctor Jacobs," Jason began, "When did you first start seeing my client?"

"Our first session was on April 12th of 2021," Jacobs answered and Jason thought the doctor's easy recall of the date without notes would send a signal to the jury about the accuracy of his testimony.

"Can you explain why Gavin became your patient three years ago?" Jason asked, using Gavin's first name, instead of 'my client', which sounded impersonal.

"He was referred to me by his family physician to help him deal with bouts of depression and melancholy that he had been suffering," Jacobs answered.

"In your sessions with Gavin, were you able to determine the reasons for these bouts?" Jason asked but before the doctor could answer, Gregory stood up and interrupted. "Your Honour, I fail to see the relevance of how the defendant was feeling three years ago to the matter before this court today."

"Your Honour, I'm asking Doctor Jacobs to provide the background that will lead up to his testimony that will be extremely relevant to my proving my client did not murder Paige Madison," Jason responded.

"On that basis, you may continue," Judge Garnet ruled and then turned to face the witness chair and said, "You can go ahead and answer the question, Doctor Jacobs."

"There were two separate issues," Jacobs said. "Gavin's business was starting to decline and he had serious doubts it could be turned around with its current structure."

"By current structure, was he talking about his partnership with Ethan Holdaway?" Jason asked.

"Yes," Jacobs answered. "Gavin said that Ethan's design work had become sloppy and clients were unhappy over the delays and the costs related to the required corrections. Gavin was not only stressed about the situation but deeply depressed because he and Ethan had been friends for a long time and had built the company together."

"Was he depressed because it was not in his nature to be confrontational and that might have to happen with his long-time partner?" Jason asked and purposely looked at the jury so they understood the importance of what he was asking. To build reasonable doubt, Jason had to show Gavin was not mentally capable of violent murder.

"Yes, he said the issue was keeping him awake at night," Jacobs responded.

"What was the other issue that was causing Gavin's depression?" Jason asked.

"His marriage," Jacobs said. "He and Alison had grown apart, especially since their two children no longer lived at home. Alison had returned to a full-time job and Gavin was working long hours, so they were seldom home together. Gavin said that both of them were no longer interested in physical intimacy with each other."

"Gavin was an unhappy man," Jason stated.

"Very much so," Jacobs responded.

"What did you do, in terms of treatment?" Jason asked next.

"We continued our sessions to discuss coping strategies and to give Gavin a sounding board for any changes in his life he might be planning," the Psychiatrist said. "As well, I prescribed low doses of Venaflaxin and Gabapentin, two anti-depressants that have been shown to work very effectively in combination."

"Now, I'm sure my colleague, Mr. Gregory, is going to ask you if it's possible these mood altering drugs you had Gavin taking could have changed his personality so that he was no longer the meek guy you described, but an aggressive individual, perhaps capable of violence," Jason said.

"Aggressive and capable of violence? Absolutely not at the low doses Gavin was taking," Jacobs answered in a firm voice. "The risk that antidepressants will incite violent or self-destructive actions has been a controversial subject since they were first introduced for human use. I've never seen it in the over thirty years I've been in practice."

"Did the antidepressants help Gavin?" Jason asked.

"He felt that they did," Jacobs answered. "During our sessions, he reported that he was sleeping better at night and feeling good during the day; calmer and less stressed."

"But then one day Gavin told you he didn't need the pills anymore," Jason said. "Why was that?"

"He told me he was in love and the happiest he had been in a long time," Jacobs answered. "He said he was seeing a young woman from his office and was planning to leave his wife so they could be together."

"And what was your reaction to his news?" Jason asked.

"Well, I tried not to ruin the obvious elation he was feeling, but I did suggest he take his time and be absolutely sure about his feelings before he made such a huge change in his life," Jacobs said.

"Did Gavin give you any details about the new lady in his life, including their substantial age difference?" Jason asked.

"Not a specific number, no, just that she was quite a bit younger," Jacobs answered. "He told me her name was Paige and she worked in the office with him."

"Doctor Jacobs, did Gavin ever give you the impression his relationship with Paige was nothing more than a middle-aged fling? A chance to have sex with a beautiful young woman? And that he would react badly, perhaps violently, if his affair was exposed?" Jason asked.

"Not at all," Jacobs stated. "I believe that Gavin was very sincere in his desire to have a permanent relationship with Paige."

"Thank you, Doctor Jacobs," Jason responded and then turned to Judge Garnet and said, "I've completed my questioning of this witness, your Honour."

"Thank you, Mr. Burke. Mr. Gregory, do you have any questions for this witness?" Judge Garnet said as he turned to look at the prosecutor.

"A few, your Honour, but I will be brief," Gregory said as he stood up behind his table, directed his attention to the Psychiatrist, and asked, "So, Doctor Jacobs, if I understand what you told this court today, you not only condoned, but supported the defendant's extramarital affair, an affair with a woman young enough to be his daughter, and lying to everyone about it, including his wife. You didn't see anything wrong with that picture?"

Jason felt that if Jacobs was fazed by Gregory's aggressive question, he didn't show it, and Jason gave him credit for that.

"It was never a case of condoning or supporting," Jacobs said calmly. "I listened very carefully to what Gavin said to me during our sessions about his relationship with Paige and pointed out the consequences to him, including the end of his marriage and possible estrangement from his adult children. Gavin assured me he was fully aware and prepared for all of that, but said that, for the first time since he was a young man, he was happy and was going to do something for himself."

"Did you know just how young Paige was?" Gregory asked.

"Not specifically. Gavin said there was a big age gap, but it didn't matter to him and Paige. Such relationships are not uncommon," Jacobs answered.

"But shortly after he told you about Paige, the defendant stopped seeing you. Is that correct?" Gregory asked.

"Yes," Jacobs answered simply.

"Well, Doctor Jacobs, according to multiple other witnesses at this trial, the defendant, Gavin Benson, was no longer the stressed, depressed, meek man you said first came to see you," Gregory said. "At the time Paige was brutally murdered, he was telling people their affair was meaningless and he was stringing Paige along, dragging his feet about leaving his wife. It would seem that he either didn't feel like fooling you anymore or your so-called safe antidepressants turned him into a lying, manipulative man capable of violence to protect his secrets."

Jason stood up quickly and exclaimed, "Your Honour, my colleague isn't asking a question, he's making an inflammatory statement!"

Judge Garnet looked sternly at the prosecutor and said, "Mr. Gregory, please reserve your comments for your summation."

"Yes, your Honour. I'm finished with this witness," Gregory said and then glanced at the jury before sitting down.

Jason saw that every member of the jury, seven men and five women, was paying close attention. No one appeared distracted or bored. There's no question Gregory is good, Jason thought, which means I'm going to have to spend even more time preparing Gavin for his testimony.

Chapter Sixteen - Present

Shane was sitting on the thin camping mattress in what he now called his cell, staring at the digital time on the face of the tablet, waiting for it to say nine o'clock, so he could email Chioma and let everyone know, most importantly Emma, that he was alive.

He had a pounding headache, his entire body ached from being tensed up, and his damaged left knee throbbed with pain. His condition was no surprise considering that he was jarred awake when Josh hit him with the ear-splitting music and intense white lights. Shane had squeezed his eyes shut as hard as he could and jammed his pointer fingers into his ears, but it seemed to do little good because his captor had turned up the intensity of the sound and light even higher than during previous sessions.

Shane wasn't sure how long the torture went on this time, it seemed like hours, and when it finally stopped, he was curled up in the fetal position on the floor, stunned, the ringing in his ears so bad it was all he could hear, and bright spots burned into his eyeballs even though he had his eyelids closed.

Shane, who had managed to keep his anger in check, couldn't this time and screamed, "You sick fuck!"

Not surprisingly, he didn't get an answer, although Shane was quite sure Josh was watching via whatever number of cameras there were in the room. He assumed Josh hit him with the lights and sound as a reminder of what would happen if he didn't do what he was told. That included the content of the first email he was being allowed to send to Chioma; no tricks, no hidden messages, just ask for the files you need.

Shane wondered, and not for the first time, if the brain tumour Josh said he had was doing something to mess up the man's ability to reason. While kidnapping Shane and forcing him to prove his father was innocent of murder might seem like a good idea to Josh, it made no sense to Shane and wouldn't to any reasonable person who thought the thing through.

Last night, after Josh said he didn't care what happened to him because he was dying, Shane asked, "What's going on Josh? What's wrong with you?"

"I have an inoperable brain tumour," Josh answered as he stood looking through the opening in the door to the room where Shane was being held. "I had suffered from headaches for years and had put them down as migraines caused by my job in the Forces. Then they started to get so bad I couldn't function and nothing I did or took would knock it down. I finally went to the doctor on base at Camp Borden, he ordered a brain scan and then he sent me to a specialist in Toronto. By the time I had the scan, the tumour was already the size of a walnut and located in an area of my brain where it can't be removed without turning me into a vegetable on a life support system."

"What's the prognosis? How long do you have?" Shane asked.

"The doctors aren't really sure," Josh answered. "The last scan showed the tumour hasn't grown, but they believe it's only temporary because the type of tumour I have is normally very aggressive. I could drop dead today or tomorrow or maybe not for six months."

"Josh, think about what you just said. If something happens to you and I'm still locked in this room, no one will find me and I will die a horrible death in here," Shane pleaded.

"Then I guess you better hurry up and figure out who really murdered Paige," Josh responded in a flat voice.

"Josh, listen to me," Shane continued to plead. "The tumour in your brain must be affecting you in such a way that you're doing something that you would normally never consider. You have to try and understand that and bring this thing to an end."

"Get some sleep and remember the rules I told you about the email You're sending tomorrow," was all Josh said and then he closed and locked the trap door.

Now, sitting on the mattress waiting to send the email, Shane thought about how he was in a nightmare that was never going to end. The digital time on the tablet hit 9 am and the dark screen disappeared, replaced by a full-screen blank email with what Shane recognized as Chioma Abiola's office address in the 'To' box. There was no 'From' line, but there was a 'Subject' box and when Shane touched it, the keyboard appeared on the screen and he simply typed, 'I'm alive and not injured'.

In the Message area, Shane wrote: 'Chioma, please reply with copies of all of my electronic files and notes on the Gavin Benson case. Do not attempt to find the source of this email or put encrypted messages, search bots or viruses in the files because my captor has advanced programs that will find them. Do not tell the police about this email. If you do any of the above, I will be killed. Tell Emma and Lan I love them. Shane Duke Daniels'.

Shane then said out loud so Josh could hear him, "If I don't sign my name that way, they won't know for sure this email is from me."

There was no send button, but the email disappeared from the screen leaving behind the digital time. Shane set the tablet beside him on the mattress and wondered what Chioma would do once she saw his email. He knew she would take a very close look at the address where it came from, but he hoped she would do as he instructed and not start digging for its source. He also knew that Chioma would be well aware of how to mask an IP address and bounce it around between different servers, so she would recognize his email for what it was. She wouldn't contact the police but would tell Jason and call Emma right away. Chioma would need their help to determine whether the email was actually from him or some crank. Shane assumed his disappearance would've been released to the public by the police looking for information about his whereabouts, so the story would have been on various sites on the internet. Chioma might think some internet troll with nothing better to do sent the email. It was the kind of thing some people did because, for reasons Shane didn't understand, it how they got their thrills.

While he waited for a reply to his email, Shane picked up the Benson trial transcript from the floor beside him and started reading through it for what seemed like the hundredth time. But it was just a show for the camera. Shane was thinking about his last conversation with Josh, specifically when the former soldier said it was possible he could drop dead at any moment. Shane had assumed right from the start there was more than a good chance he would not be leaving this room alive and the unpredictability of Josh's behaviour because of his brain tumour confirmed the worse case scenario.

Shane had been mentally working his way through a plan to escape, but a lot of things had to go just right for it to have any chance of working. It primarily depended on Shane's acting ability and the hope that his brain tumour had not erased all of Josh's compassion. But Shane knew that even with a high probability of failure, he had to attempt to escape as soon as possible before it was too late.

Chapter Eighteen - Present

Ariel Durst lived in an older four-storey brick apartment building on a mostly residential street off King George Road.

Emma parked her SUV in a visitor's spot at the back of the building and walked into the small area between the front door and the inner security entrance. There were numbered mailboxes on the right wall and on the left, a keyboard where you entered a number to call the tenant you were there to see. Luckily, the landlord had kept the system simple; all the numbers started with one followed by three digits, which Emma assumed were apartment numbers. The number beside A. Durst meant Ariel was on the fourth floor.

She could simply punch in the number and call Ariel's apartment, but Emma wasn't sure if the young woman would let her in after she tried to explain who she was and what she wanted. Emma thought it was a safe bet that Ariel wouldn't be interested in dredging up the death of her best friend and what she went through on the stand at the Benson trial.

Then Emma got lucky when an elderly lady carrying a shopping bag walked in, held a plastic card against a small black box beside the inner door and it clicked open. Emma quickly stepped over and with a smile on her face held the door open for the woman, who smiled back, said thank you, and walked in with Emma following.

The elderly lady went down the hallway to a first floor unit and Emma took the elevator to the fourth and knocked on the door of Ariel's apartment. There was no answer and Emma was about to knock again when the door opened against the security chain and the face of a pretty young woman appeared.

"Can I help you?" Ariel asked cautiously.

"Ariel, my name is Emma Carstairs and my partner is Shane Daniels, the investigator for the defence lawyer in the Gavin Benson trial," Emma said and before she could explain any further, Ariel asked, "How did you get in here? What do you want?"

"Shane is missing, possibly kidnapped, and I believe it may be connected to Paige's murder and the Benson trial," Emma said. "I have a couple of questions for you that could help find him."

"I'm sorry your partner is missing, but I don't see how I can help," Ariel said and then added, "I need to get ready for work," before starting to close the door.

Emma reached out with her hand, held the door open, and pleaded, "Please, Ariel, it's really important, I need your help, it won't take long. Please."

Ariel hesitated and looked at Emma, saw the sincerity on her face, undid the security chain, opened the door, and retreated into the apartment. Emma followed her into a spacious living room, tastefully decorated with a leather sofa and easy chair, glass coffee table, small china cabinet and a deep area rug. A glass sliding door with vertical blinds led to a small balcony overlooking a park.

Ariel didn't ask Emma to sit and instead stood facing her with her arms crossed. She was dressed in a nicely tailored, dark blue pantsuit, her long dark hair pulled back and tied in a ponytail.

"You have a beautiful apartment," Emma said with a smile, trying to break the ice.

"Thanks, so how can I help? I don't want to be late for work," Ariel said, impatience obvious in her voice.

Emma reached into the back pocket of her jeans, took out her phone, called up a picture she had stored on it, and then held the phone out in front of her so Ariel could see the screen.

"Do you know this guy?" Emma asked.

"Sure, that's Logan Stewart, I went to high school with him," Ariel answered and then asked, "What about him?"

"I was hoping you could tell me something about him," Emma replied.

"First you need to tell me why you're interested in him," Ariel said.

Emma explained that Logan attended every minute of the Benson trial and she believed that he was the one who made unwanted posts to the Facebook page that Ariel and Emily Watson had set up in memory of Paige. Emma said there was a very strong possibility her partner Shane's disappearance was linked to Paige's murder and the

Benson trial, and she needed to check on anyone connected to the case who might have a motive to harm Shane.

"What, you think Logan had something to do with Paige's murder?" Ariel asked. "The man who did it is already in prison."

"Gavin Benson committed suicide in his cell," Emma said.

"Oh, I didn't know. I was hoping the bastard would rot in jail," Ariel said with some anger in her voice.

"The thing is, Ariel, I don't think Shane was convinced Benson killed Paige," Emma continued. "One of my theories is that Shane continued to investigate Paige's murder even after the trial ended and it led him to Logan. It's possible he confronted Logan and Logan did something to him."

"You think Logan killed him?" Ariel asked.

"As much as it hurts to think that, it's possible, but I'm hoping otherwise," Emma said, some emotion creeping into her voice. What can you tell me about Logan," she then asked.

Ariel then told Emma that he didn't start that way, but by the end of high school, Logan had turned into a bit of a creep. He always had a crush on Paige, even back when they went to elementary school, and would often follow her around like a lost puppy. Paige put up with it because he was basically a good guy and she thought he was kinda cute with his curly red hair and freckles.

"So when did he turn into a creep?" Emma asked.

"When we got into high school, Logan was never far away from wherever Paige was and somehow he managed to be in most of her classes," Ariel explained. "Starting in Grade eleven, he started asking Paige out all the time. She kept turning him down, but at that time, as I said, he was still basically a good guy. Being the kind of person she was, Paige felt sorry for him, so she eventually said yes and they went out on one date, to a movie they both wanted to see, if I remember correctly."

"So, it was just one date, but Logan didn't give up?" Emma asked.

"No. During our senior year, Paige finally took him aside and told him she was not at all interested in him romantically and if he wanted to remain her friend, he had to back off," Ariel said.

"But he didn't," Emma stated.

Ariel said it was after Paige talked to him that Logan started acting creepy. Paige told her that while he stopped hanging around close to her at school, she saw him on numerous occasions driving by her parent's house in an old Ford Taurus Logan's parents bought him and she thought he was following her when she was at the mall. Paige had to remove him as a friend from her Facebook because of some of the very personal comments he was posting about how she looked and dressed, and about how some people deny their true feelings about others.

"Did Paige ever consider reporting Logan to the police as a stalker?" Emma asked.

"I tried to get her to do it a bunch of times," Ariel responded. "But she wouldn't do it. She didn't want to get Logan in trouble. I kept telling her she was too nice for her own good."

"When Page was murdered, why didn't you tell the police about Logan?" Emma asked, trying not to look how she felt; that this young woman standing in front of her had failed to provide some important information to investigators.

"I didn't need to because they arrested Benson right away," Ariel said in a defensive tone, which told Emma she had failed to keep a look of disdain off her face. She didn't want to anger Ariel and get kicked out of the apartment before she got the information she needed, so she quickly moved on.

"Were you aware that Logan was fixated with the Benson trial and was in the courtroom every day?" Emma asked.

"I saw him sitting off by himself during the few times I could attend because I wasn't working," Ariel answered. "We didn't acknowledge each other because he knew how I felt about him."

"Do you know anything about his current personal life, like where he lives?" Emma asked.

"I heard he got married, but it didn't last, and I'm not sure when it was, maybe six months ago, I saw him at Walmart with one of those yellow vests employees wear so I assume he was working there," Ariel said. "I think someone told me that after his marriage broke up, he moved back in with his parents."

"Do you know their address?" Emma asked next.

"Sure, Paige and I, and some of our friends used to hang around at Logan's parent's place when we were kids. I assume they live in the same place," Ariel said and then added, "Give me your phone number and I'll text you the address."

After that was done, Emma said, "I'll let you get to work. Thanks for the information," and then walked to the door of the apartment to leave.

"Just so you know, if I thought for a minute that Logan had anything to do with Paige's murder, I would have said something," Ariel said to Emma's back. "He's a creep but I always thought he was harmless. Besides, I just know that Benson did it."

I wonder what else you knew and didn't bother to mention to anyone, Emma thought but didn't say out loud. Instead, she didn't say anything, just walked out of the apartment, closing the door behind her.

On the way down the elevator, Emma told herself she should be calling Sargent Lucas of Missing Persons, informing him about Logan Stewart, and letting the police check the guy out. But Emma didn't want to wait. If there was any chance at all that Shane was still alive and Stewart had him, she was going to find out right now.

Chapter Nineteen - The Trial

It was a case of so far, so good, for Jason as he hesitated momentarily in his questioning of Gavin Benson to take a sip from the glass of water sitting on the defence table beside him. The courtrooms in the historic building were notoriously dry and everyone, from the Judge to the Clerks, went through gallons of water throughout a trial.

Gavin looked poised as he sat in the witness chair, sitting up straight, hands in his lap. Jason had told him not to cross his legs because that would make him appear too casual to the jury when he was talking about Paige's death. Gavin was well groomed, Jason had arranged a haircut in the holding cell and was wearing a charcoal suit, white shirt and blue tie with no pattern. Jason wanted him to look like the respected, successful businessman that he was.

So far, Jason had Gavin talk about his personal background; his family growing up, his education, how he met and married Alison, his two children, Josh and Melissa, and how he and Ethan Holdaway had started and grown their business.

Jason wanted the jury to like Gavin and hopefully see him as an ordinary middle-aged man who was forced to deal with personal issues that anyone could relate to; financial challenges caused by the stalled economy during the COVID pandemic and bouts of depression and self-doubt.

"You started seeing Doctor Jacobs and he prescribed some anti-depressants as well as providing counselling," Jason said to Gavin.

"Yes, and it was some help," Gavin said. "At least I was sleeping at night. But the tension at home because of my failing relationship with Alison and the stress at work was still crushing me."

"And then you found yourself in an intimate relationship with Paige Madison," Jason said and then asked, "How did that start?"

"At first, I thought it was just some innocent flirtation on Paige's part," Gavin said. "I enjoyed it because Paige was not only a beautiful woman, but was intelligent and well-spoken. I was attracted to her, and not just physically, but I was sure she had that effect on a lot of men and I never expected in a million years that she would feel the same way about me, a married, middle-aged man old enough to be her father."

"But it turned out you were wrong, that Paige had fallen in love with you," Jason said.

"It was a shock, a delightful shock," Gavin responded. "We were alone in my office one day going over some paperwork when she asked me if I knew why she flirted with me. I wasn't sure what to say but before I could come up with an answer, she said she was doing it to try and get my attention and see if there was any chance I was interested in her. I still didn't know what to say. She then told me she couldn't wait any longer for me to make some kind of move, that she had fallen in love with me and hoped I felt the same way."

"And you did," Jason prompted.

"I can't explain it, but when I was with Paige it was as if someone had lifted an anvil off my shoulders," Gavin said. "Suddenly, my personal and financial issues were not squeezing the life out of me and no longer seemed insurmountable."

"Did you and Paige discuss the consequences of your relationship?" Jason asked.

"Many times," Gavin answered. "I asked Paige if she was sure she wanted to be with an old man when she was still relatively young and she said she didn't care. She then asked if I was prepared for the end of my marriage and the likely negative reaction from my son and daughter, as well as from my friends and colleagues. And I told her I also didn't care. We were deeply in love and were not going to let anything stand in the way of being together."

"My colleague, the prosecutor, will no doubt ask you why you denied the nature of your relationship with Paige when you were confronted about it by your partner, Ethan Holdaway. Can you tell us why?" Jason asked. He took a quick glance at the jury and noted they were paying close attention, realizing the importance of the conversation between the two business partners to what the Crown contended was Gavin's motive to murder Paige.

"I admit I panicked at first when Ethan asked about what was going on between Paige and I," Gavin said. "I knew the conversation was coming, eventually, but I guess I wasn't ready. It was a knee-jerk reaction which I regret."

"Did you blame Paige for initiating the affair and tell Ethan you would take care of it?" Jason asked.

"I never told Ethan I blamed Paige, that never happened, I don't know why he said that," Gavin answered firmly but in a normal tone of voice. Jason had warned Gavin several times when they were preparing for his testimony that he had to keep his emotions, specifically his anger, in check when answering questions, especially from the prosecutor. Jason told Gavin to save any emotional responses for when he talked about Paige.

"But you did say you would take care of it," Jason stated.

"I did say that, yes, because I wanted to cut our conversation short," Gavin admitted, "As I said, I panicked because I wasn't ready yet to deal with the impact in the office of my relationship with Paige. I hadn't told my wife yet and I felt that was a lot more important than getting into it with Ethan."

"You don't think you came across to your partner as angry and prepared to do whatever it took to make Paige and your affair with her go away?" Jason asked.

"Absolutely not!" Gavin exclaimed.

"Why would Ethan testify that's what happened?" Jason asked. It was one of the questions he and Gavin had gone over very carefully in their preparatory meetings.

"He's putting everything on me to shield himself from any possible legal action which might occur as a result of this trial, such as a lawsuit," Gavin said.

"Your Honour," Gregory said as he stood up behind his table. "The defendant cannot possibly know Mr. Holdaway's thought process and should not be allowed to speculate."

"I agree," Judge Garnet ruled and then turned and said to Gavin, "Mr. Benson, please keep your opinions about what other people might be thinking to yourself."

The Judge then looked at Jason and said, "Mr. Burke, you know better than to ask a question that allows a witness to speculate."

"I apologize, your Honour," Jason said, trying to sound contrite, but he could tell by the way Garnet was glaring at him that the Judge didn't buy it and that he knew what Jason was doing was on purpose for the benefit of the jury.

Garnet then turned his attention to the jury and said, "Members of the jury, you will disregard the last statement made by the witness because it's speculation and has no basis in fact."

Jason knew it was impossible for the jurors to forget what Gavin just said about his partner. Human nature didn't work that way. Jason had accomplished what he wanted; putting a dent in Ethan Holdaway's credibility as a witness.

"You may continue questioning your witness, Mr. Burke, but I'm warning you to be careful because my patience is wearing thin," Judge Garnet said to Jason.

"Yes, your Honour," Jason responded and then turned to Gavin and said, "Her friend, Ariel Durst, testified that Paige intended to tell you she was pregnant on the morning she was killed. But for some reason, she didn't, and you didn't know until you were told by the police. Any idea why she didn't tell you that day?"

"I don't know," Gavin said. "We made love and spent some quiet time together. Perhaps she didn't want to spoil the moment. We never did spend any time discussing what was ahead once we went public with our relationship."

"Do you think she was afraid to tell you?" Jason asked.

"It's possible she was worried about how I would feel about becoming a father again at my age," Gavin answered.

"And how would you have felt if you knew? Angry, as is being suggested by the prosecution?" Jason asked.

"No, not at all!" Gavin exclaimed. "Sure, it would have given me pause when I thought about being a father again at my age and the fact I would be quite elderly by the time my son or daughter was a teenager. But all of that wouldn't have mattered because I loved Paige and would have loved starting a family with her."

"Gavin, did you murder Paige?" Jason asked.

As he had told him to do, Gavin looked directly at the jury and said, "No, I did not. I was in love with Paige and would never hurt her. I'm heartbroken about her death and think about her every day."

"Thank you, Gavin," Jason responded and then turning to Judge Garnet, he said, "I've finished questioning this witness, your Honour."

As he returned to his table, Jason thought to himself that Gavin's testimony had gone well, perhaps better than he expected. The most important thing was that Gavin kept his emotions in check because Jason knew firsthand that his client had a temper plus witnesses had testified about it earlier in the trial. Now, Gavin needed to do the same thing during what he expected to be an aggressive cross-examination by the prosecutor who needed to break down Gavin's story to prove to the jury he had a motive to kill Paige.

Once he was back at the defence table, and while he waited for Gregory to begin questioning Gavin, Jason studied the jury. He considered himself to be very good at reading faces and had used the skill many times over the years to catch witnesses lying when they were on the stand. But this jury was an enigma to him. They had all been paying close attention to the proceedings since the start of the trial and Jason gave them a lot of credit for that because sitting on a murder trial jury is not easy; the days can be long, some of the testimony can be tedious, and there's a lot of pressure to make the right decision.

During the presentation of the Crown's case, Jason had watched both the facial expressions and physical tics of the jurors very closely, trying to get a sense of how they were reacting to what they heard. Most certainly, the majority showed signs of being upset as they heard the details of what was done to Paige when she was killed and many of them stared at Gavin with disgust evident on their faces. But aside from that, the men and women on the panel, of various ages and backgrounds, remained fairly stoic during the rest of the testimony. It made it very difficult for Jason to get a handle on how they were reacting to what they were hearing and he was concerned that many of them had already made up their mind that Gavin was guilty and had little interest in anything he was trying to do to raise reasonable doubt.

Jason's thoughts were interrupted when Judge Garnet said, "Mr. Gregory, you may begin your cross-examination of this witness."

Jason knew that how Gavin handled the expected tough questions from the prosecutor would be the most critical time of the trial.

Gregory got up from behind his table, went and stood about halfway to the witness stand, and began by asking, "Mr. Benson, if you didn't murder Paige Madison, why did you say to the police officer who brought you in for questioning, 'I did this to Paige?'"

Jason knew this question was coming and while he could have dealt with Gavin's statement to police during his questioning to try and soften its impact, he decided it was better not to draw attention to it twice. Let the prosecutor ask and get it over with quickly.

Gavin's statement, 'I did this to Paige', was the subject of a long debate during the voir dire portion of the trial as Jason tried, unsuccessfully, to prevent the officer who heard it from testifying. Gregory argued what Gavin said was a spontaneous, excited utterance known in the law as 'res gestae', a traditional class of exemption to the hearsay rule. The rule says a statement relating to a 'startling event or condition' can be admitted in a trial when the person saying it is under the stress of excitement over what happened. The 'excited utterance' exception generally applied to a statement made to a police officer which was not in response to a question.

As well, Gregory claimed that when Gavin made the statement he had just arrived at the police station for questioning and was not yet considered a suspect or was advised he was under arrest, so the officer was not obligated yet to advise Benson of his rights. While Canada doesn't have the 'Miranda Warning' that most people are familiar with from American crime shows, our law does have similar rights to protect people in custody and under interrogation. They're known, in short, as 'Charter Rights' guaranteed under the Canadian Charter of Rights and Freedoms and like Miranda, police must advise you of your right to remain silent and your right to a lawyer.

Before Gavin could answer Gregory's question, Jason stood up and said, "Your Honour, for the trial record, I would again voice my objection to allowing what my client said to a police officer before he was advised of his Charter Rights. No matter what my colleague claims, Mr. Benson was already considered the prime suspect in Paige's murder when he was picked up and taken to the police station for questioning. He should have been advised of his rights before they even put him in the cruiser."

Jason had also made the same objection earlier in the trial before the testimony of the officer who heard what Gavin said.

"Mr. Burke, your objection has already been noted once in this trial and my ruling still stands," Judge Garnet stated and then turned to Gavin in the witness box and said, "Please answer the question, Mr. Benson."

"I was very upset when I said that," Gavin answered. "I had just been told that Paige was murdered and her body found in a field. I was in shock and thinking maybe Paige's death had something to do with our relationship."

"Who would care enough about your secret December-May affair to kill Paige except for you, Mr. Benson?" Gregory asked pointedly.

"I don't know. I don't know what I was thinking. As I said, I was in shock," Gavin responded.

"It sounded like a confession," Gregory stated.

"It was not a confession!" Gavin said emphatically. "I did not kill Paige. I loved her."

"So you keep saying, Mr. Benson, but if that's true, why did you lie all the time about your relationship?" Gregory asked. "You never told your wife like you said you were going to do and you lied to your partner. You told him your affair with Paige was meaningless and even blamed her for starting it."

"I have already said I did not tell Ethan that I blamed Paige. That never happened," Gavin said.

"So you claim. But you do admit you said, 'I'll take care of it'" Gregory said.

"I said that yes, but as I told Mr. Burke a few minutes ago, I said that to try and cut my conversation with Ethan short," Gavin stated.

"Is that really why you said that, Mr. Benson?" Gregory asked and then said, "Isn't it more likely, based on what we've heard at this trial, that you realized your sexual escapade with a pretty girl young enough to be your daughter was being exposed and it was going to destroy your marriage and maybe wreck your business. And to make matters worse, Paige tells you she's pregnant. You decide you have to get her out of your life, so you kill her, violate her body and dump her in a field to make it look like she was the victim of a random killer."

"Your Honour," Jason said as he stood up. "Is my colleague making his summation or asking a question? A question, I might add, that my client has already answered."

"Move on, Mr. Gregory," Judge Garnet said to the prosecutor.

"Mr. Benson," Gregory said as he took a step closer to the witness box. "You were cheating on your wife, you lied to your partner about the nature of your relationship with Paige and you initially lied to the police. Why should members of the jury believe anything you say?"

"I am not lying when I say I didn't kill Paige and that we were in love and planned to spend the rest of our lives together," Gavin said with conviction in his voice.

"So you claim," Gregory stated flatly, turned to the Judge and said, "I'm finished with this witness your Honour."

"Any re-direct, Mr. Burke?" Garnet asked Jason.

"No, your Honour," Jason answered. He had decided it was time to get Gavin off the stand. He felt his client's testimony had gone about how he had expected and overall, thought Gavin had done pretty well dealing with Gregory's aggressive cross-examination. He didn't lose his temper and, for the most part, stayed calm.

Still, it had gone against Jason's instinct to allow Gavin to testify in the first place, even though he knew it was necessary. After Gavin left the witness chair and returned to sit beside him, Jason again looked at the jury, trying to get some sense of how they were reacting to Gavin's testimony. He still couldn't get a read off any of their faces.

The one thing that Jason did know for sure was that the trial had basically come down to whether the jury believed what Gavin said about his relationship with Paige or if they thought he was lying and was a cold-blooded killer.

Chapter Twenty - Present

Logan Stewart's parent's home was a small, older brick bungalow on a street lined with maple trees in Brantford's east end. The lots the homes in the area sat on were narrow and long, fenced in and well-maintained.

I wouldn't mind living in this neighbourhood, Emma thought, as she parked her SUV in front of the Stewart's house. Emma was purposely thinking about something other than the reason she was here to try and keep herself calm, which she knew was going to be important went she confronted Logan. If there was any chance he was involved in Shane's disappearance or perhaps in Paige Madison's murder, she had to find out.

Emma walked to the front door and didn't see a doorbell, so she knocked on the outer screen door. She could feel her heart thumping rapidly. Calm, be calm, she told herself, as an elderly, gray-haired woman opened the inside door. She was small and thin, with a heavily wrinkled pale face, wearing oversized glasses with light purple frames.

"Can I help you? If you're a Jehovah's Witness, I'm not interested," the woman said.

"No, I'm not," Emma said with a smile. "Mrs. Stewart, I was wondering if your son Logan was home?"

"What do you want with him?" the woman asked suspiciously.

"It's a personal matter," Emma answered, maintaining the smile on her face.

"A personal matter? Well, he's got lots of those," the elderly woman responded. "You better come in then," she said and opened the screen door so Emma could walk by her and into the small open area at the front of the house.

To Emma's left there was an opening to the living room with some well worn furniture and on her right a small area with a heavy looking wood dining table, four fancy high-back chairs, and a beautiful tall china cabinet. Straight ahead, Emma saw a hallway leading to the kitchen, stairs to the second floor and a door she assumed led to the basement.

Leaving Emma standing at the front, the elderly woman walked over to that door, opened it, and yelled, "Logan, are you awake?! There's a very pretty woman here that wants to see you! On a personal matter, she says!"

A young man still living at home in his parent's basement. How stereotypical was that? Emma asked herself.

"Who is it?! I'm not expecting anybody," Emma heard a male voice call out from the basement.

"I don't know who it is!" the woman yelled down the stairs and then turned to Emma and asked, "What's your name?"

"It's Emma. Tell Logan it's important I talk to him," Emma replied.

"Her name's Emma and she says she has something important to talk to you about!" Mrs. Stewart yelled.

"I don't know any Emmas! Tell her I'm busy," Logan yelled back.

"For Christ's sake, Logan! Don't be rude! Just get your ass up here and talk to the lady!" Mrs. Stewart called down the stairs in an even louder voice than before.

There was silence and then Emma heard footsteps coming up the stairs. When Logan emerged from the doorway to the basement, she saw right away that he no longer resembled his high school yearbook photo. He was rail thin, the arms hanging out of the Hulk t-shirt he was wearing looked like sticks, and his gray sweatpants were barely staying up. His face looked sunken, his pasty complexion made the freckles on his face stand out, he had dark circles under his bloodshot eyes, and the curly red hair that was so prominent in earlier photos was flat against his scalp, greasy and tangled.

This guy was no stranger to the pipe, Emma concluded right away. She was very familiar with the look of someone who was a heavy drug user. Many of the recent amputees that Emma counselled as a volunteer had already developed serious booze and drug habits by the time she saw them. The loss of a limb was a life-changing event and some people fell into a deep depression, sometimes turning to alcohol and drugs to try and cope.

"You can talk in the living room and I'll go to the kitchen," Mrs. Stewart said and then walked away.

Logan went into the living, his hands deep in the pockets of his sweatpants, and Emma followed. He turned to face her, didn't offer her a chance to sit down, and asked, "I don't know you, do I? What do you want?"

"My name is Emma Carstairs," Emma said and then took her phone out of the back pocket of her jeans, called up a picture of Shane, and held it out for Logan to look at.

"This is my partner, Shane Daniels. Has he been here to talk to you over the past couple of days?" She asked.

Logan took a brief glance at the phone and said, "I've never seen this guy. Sorry." He then added, "Anything else? I'm kinda busy."

"Are you sure you've never seen him before?" Emma insisted.

"I already said, lady, I don't know him," Logan said and Emma could see in his face his complete disinterest in their conversation.

That's when Emma lost it. Her fear that Shane was dead, a lack of sleep and her frayed nerves all boiled to the surface as anger. She reached out and grabbed Logan by the throat, squeezed hard, and pushed him backwards until his legs hit the edge of the couch and he was forced to sit down. Bending over him, Emma kept her hand gripped on Logan's throat and put her face close to his.

"You want to try again you stupid crackhead!" Emma exclaimed in a low, threatening voice. "You would have seen him many times in the same courtroom where you sat every day during the Benson trial. And now he's missing and because you're lying to me about never seeing him before, I think you know something about it or maybe you're responsible."

Logan had a terrified look on his face and his eyes were bulging as Emma kept the pressure on his neck. He reached up with both hands and tried desperately to pull off Emma's iron grip. Emma felt her anger start to dissipate and the hot flush on her face cool. She released her grip and backed away from the couch.

"You ready to start over, Logan," she said calmly, "Or will I have to punch the shit out of you, which I am more than prepared to do."

"Okay, Okay! calm down!" Logan said in a hoarse voice, his right hand covering his now sore throat. "I do remember seeing him a few times at the trial sitting on the bench behind the defence table. But that's the last time I saw him, I swear to God!"

"He's never been here to talk to you about Paige Madison's murder?" Emma asked.

"No! I've already told you I've never talked to the guy!" Logan rasped.

"Because you lied to me, I'm having a hard time believing anything coming out of your mouth," Emma said. "Even though he was found guilty by a jury, I think Shane wasn't convinced Gavin Benson killed Paige and while he was continuing his investigation, he started taking a serious look at you."

Emma pointed at Logan's face and then continued, "Shane probably wondered why a guy Paige went to school with would sit through every minute of the Benson trial. And then, just like I did, Shane found out your feelings about Paige had turned you into her stalker, plus you were trolling her on the internet. I think Shane started to believe that it was actually you who killed Paige and did horrible things to her body because you found out she was having an affair with an older man. It made you jealous and angry. You were at the trial every day because you either had a guilty conscience or because you took delight in seeing someone else take the blame for Paige's murder. Shane came here to ask you some questions. You panicked and did something to him."

"That's bullshit!" Logan croaked, holding his hands up in front of his face out of fear Emma was going to choke him again. "I would never hurt Paige. I've loved her ever since we were little kids. I didn't kill her and I haven't seen your boyfriend since the end of the trial."

Emma took another threatening step toward Logan who turned his body sideways and covered his head with his arms.

"Maybe you were strung out on drugs and don't remember what you did. Maybe you should show me your basement lair in case there's something there that proves you're lying to me," Emma said as she leaned threateningly over Logan, but she was now convinced, based on his reaction to her confrontation, that Logan was telling the truth.

"I think you need to leave now, lady," Emma suddenly heard and turned to see Logan's mom walking into the living room.

"I should call the cops and have you arrested for threatening my son," the elderly woman declared.

"You can do that, Mrs. Stewart," Emma responded. "But then I will tell the officer in charge of investigating my partner's disappearance everything I know about your drug-addicted son. He'll then get a search warrant for your basement and I'm sure he'll find all kinds of illegal stuff, like perhaps your son's crack stash or a computer with some interesting files on it."

"It's okay, just let it go, Mom," Logan said, the panic obvious in his still raspy voice.

Without saying another word, Emma walked out of the house and got in her vehicle, where she sat with her hands on the steering wheel, taking long, slow deep breaths. I tried to stay calm, but I lost my temper anyway, Emma admonished herself. I could have seriously injured that sick young man and got myself arrested. A lot of good I could've done to help find Shane if I was in jail. Stupid! Stupid! Stupid! Emma screamed in her head as she pounded the steering wheel with her right hand.

Her anger at herself now dissipated, Emma sat back in the driver's seat and started thinking about her next steps. She was definitely going to call Sergeant Lucas of Missing Persons and talk to him about Logan Stewart and hopefully, he'll take the drug-addled young man in for questioning as well as search the basement of his house.

Although Emma tended to believe Logan's denials while she threatened him with physical harm about being involved in Paige's murder and Shane's disappearance, she knew that many addicts were accomplished liars. Logan most certainly checked off a lot of boxes; he had a lifelong infatuation with Paige but she wanted nothing to do with him, and if he killed her, Shane coming around asking questions would be a threat to his secret.

Emma decided she would drive home and see if Ben and Michelle had discovered any new information. First, she took her phone out of the back pocket of her jeans to check for any emails or texts that might have come in while she was in the house. She had put the phone on silent so it wouldn't go off when she was confronting Logan.

There were three missed calls and a text message. Emma opened the text first and saw it was from Chioma at Burke and Associates. It said: 'Emma, where are you? You need to come to the office right away. We think we've heard from Shane. He may be alive!'

Oh my God! Emma thought as she started her vehicle. Please let it be him!

Chapter Twenty One - Present

Shane sat on his mattress looking down at the notes he had made from the trial transcripts and watching the tablet beside him for a reply to the email he sent Chioma.

He wasn't expecting a response right away because Chioma would first show it to Jason and they would try to determine if it was actually from him or from someone trying to get their kicks by posing as him. Shane was sure that once he saw the middle name, Duke, that he had used at the end of the email, Jason would know it was authentic.

Jason, Emma and Ben were three of the very few people Shane had reluctantly told what his middle name was because over the years he had grown to hate it since it reminded him of his late father, the convicted killer, the man who betrayed him and ruined the once happy memories he had of his youth. When Shane was a young boy, his father told him he wanted to name him 'Duke', the nickname for movie star John Wayne. His father was a huge fan of Western films, especially anything starring Wayne, and when he was growing up, Shane and his dad spent hours watching old westerns on TV. But, his father told him, his mother refused to have a son named 'Duke', so they compromised. She agreed to 'Shane', the name of the main character in the movie of the same name starring Alan Ladd, and 'Duke' as his middle name.

There would also be a delay before he saw any return email from Chioma because Josh would study it very closely, looking for any possible hidden message in the text or something embedded in the files designed to pinpoint his location. He would open the attachments and look through every file very carefully to make sure they contained only notes related to his father's case.

For his attempt to escape to work, Shane had to believe that Josh would be somewhere in the building which included the room where he was being held captive, likely sitting in front of a laptop, either waiting for the return email or if it came in, studying it. Perhaps he had more than one computer, the other to monitor what the cameras were showing in Shane's room and to provide the audio from the hidden microphones.

I'm going to need my best acting skills, Shane thought, and hope that Josh's diseased brain hadn't changed him so much that he wouldn't come and help him if it looked like he was in serious medical distress. If nothing else, he hoped Josh would come into the room to see what was wrong out of fear Shane would be incapacitated before he did what the former soldier wanted.

Here we go, Shane said to himself, as he let the papers he was holding drop out of his hands, wrapped his arms around his midsection and started moaning like he was in pain. He went down on his side, curled up in the fetal position, and continued to make noises like he was suffering severe cramps.

"Josh, I need help, there's something wrong with me!" Shane called out, making his voice sound strained. "My guts on are fire! I feel like my heart is going to burst out of my chest! Please, at least bring me some water!"

Shane went back to his moaning, his face scrunched up, his lips parted so that if Josh was watching on his monitors, he could see that Shane was gritting his teeth in pain.

"Hang on," Shane heard Josh say over the speaker.

To be fully convincing and to get Josh into the room to check on him, Shane had to time his next move just right. When he was a kid and he didn't feel like going to school, Shane became proficient at vomiting on demand. It took practice and a lot of failed painful attempts, but eventually, he had his gag reflex trained so that as soon as he put two fingers down his throat, up would come the contents of his stomach. It had been more than a few decades since Shane last stuck his fingers down his throat, but he was counting on his gag reflex having a long memory.

Assuming that Josh was going to at least open the trap door, take a look at him and drop a bottle of water into the room, Shane listened for the sound of the latch being turned. When he heard it, he hoped for the best, or in this case the worst, and jammed two fingers deep into his throat.

It worked! Just as he heard the sound of the trap door falling open and hitting the main door, he threw up the contents of his stomach on the floor beside him; the toast and lukewarm coffee Josh had given him for breakfast. As soon as that was done, he screwed up his face, returned to the fetal position and started shaking his entire body.

"Son of a bitch!" Shane heard Josh exclaim and to his relief, heard the sound of the deadbolt being slid open on the door. Shane continued to shake his body and prepared himself for what he had to do next. As soon as he felt Josh's hand on his shoulder, Shane opened his eyes so he could see where he was aiming, uncoiled his body to give him momentum, and punched Josh in the throat. Shane wanted to incapacitate Josh, but he knew he was running the risk of crushing his hyoid bone and if that happened, his captor would choke to death.

Josh fell back onto the floor from his kneeling position and grabbed his throat with both hands as he struggled to breathe. Shane got to his feet and started for the door, but his damaged knee gave out and he fell hard onto the concrete.

Not now! Shane exclaimed to himself as searing pain shot from his knee up the entire left side of his body and he felt a trickle of blood running down the side of his face from where he hit his head.

Got to get up! Got to get out! Shane admonished himself, pushed up with his arms, and stood with all of his weight on his right leg. As he tried to put his left foot on the floor to balance himself, he heard

Josh coughing and when he looked over his shoulder, he saw that Josh was trying to get to his feet.

Faced with no choice, Shane started hopping on his right leg in an effort to get through the door before Josh got his hands on him. His momentum was propelling him forward as he hopped, but he was also losing his balance and as he was going through the doorway, he put his arms out to cushion his fall as he went down to the floor. He rolled a couple of times to make sure he was clear of the door, sat up as fast as he could, and pushed the heavy wooden door closed. He reached up and just as he engaged the deadbolt, the door shuddered as Josh slammed into it.

"You son of a bitch, I'm going to fucking kill you!" Josh rasped through the door and then started pounding on it with his fist. "You lied to me! You had no intention of doing the right thing and clearing my father's name! For that, when I get out of here, you're a dead man!" Josh screamed as his voice got stronger.

While Josh continued to hammer on the door, Shane took a look around and saw, as he had suspected, that he was in the basement of a building, likely a house. The two-by-four framing of the wall Josh had built to form the room Shane was kept in was facing him, leaving just a small area with stairs leading to the main floor. There was a small junction box attached to the wall near the floor and both a heavy electrical wire and coax cable ran from the box and up the side of the stairs.

He spent a lot of money and time putting this cell together for me, Shane thought, a sign of Josh's determination to prove his father's innocence, although he had chosen a nonsensical way to go about it, probably caused by the tumour in his brain.

Shane slowly got to his feet and tried to put a bit of weight on his left leg. His knee was still on fire with pain, but at least he could now stand, so he hobbled over to the bottom of the stairs. To play it safe in case his leg gave out again, Shane decided to crawl up the stairs. He noted that Josh had stopped yelling and banging on the door.

At the top of the stairs, Shane used the door frame to steady himself as he stood up and saw that he was in the kitchen of a house, an old one by the look of the room. There were old-fashioned dark green wooden cupboards that appeared to have been painted by hand many times over the years. The dirty countertop was littered with cardboard boxes and tools, and beside the sink, there was a small hand pump that would have been used to draw fresh water from a well. The floor was yellowed, cracked linoleum and in the middle of the room, there was an old wooden table and a single chair.

As Shane had suspected, two laptops were sitting open on the table. Josh had smashed one of the receptacles out of the wall so he could direct wire a plate of multiple outlets to provide electricity to the computers and to a unit that looked like a sound mixing board, likely used to control the intense lights and ear-splitting music in the room downstairs.

The first thing Shane looked for was a cell phone, but there was nothing on the table, which meant that Josh had it with him. There was a cardboard box on the floor beside the table filled with fast food bags and containers, and in one corner Shane could see the smashed remains of his phone from which Josh would have removed and destroyed the SIM card to prevent the phone from being traced.

Shane sat down at the table, it felt good to get off his bad knee, and he looked at the screens on the laptops. On one he could see Josh in the basement room, sitting on the mattress with his hands covering his face, and on the other some kind of program was open which was a complete mystery to Shane. He assumed it was some type of encryption program Josh was using to mask his location or to search anything coming into the computer for viruses and search worms. Shane clicked to leave the program and return to the home screen, hoping there would be a standard email program he could use to contact Emma and let her know he was okay, as well as Google or some type of internet search engine. Google was there, but he didn't recognize any of the other icons, nothing that looked like it might be for email. He did not doubt that double-clicking one of the icons would lead to the program Josh was using to constantly change his IP address.

Shane decided to try Google and see if he could find out where the hell he was or maybe use Facebook or Instagram to get a message to Emma, who in turn could contact the police. He clicked on Google Maps to see if it would show the area he was in, but what came up appeared to be a map of a section of New York City as Josh had his system switching to different servers to hide his location. As he was about to call up and log into his Messenger account to try and get a note to Emma, something on the table sticking out from behind the laptop's monitor caught his eye. It was the end of a car key. Shane reached around the front of the laptop and picked up what turned out to be several keys on a Toronto Maple Leafs key ring. Shane smiled as he looked at what he had in his hand; the keys to his Charger! The car must be on the property somewhere and that meant he could drive away from here and try and find his way home. Shane put the keys in his pants pocket and slowly limped across the kitchen, into a narrow hallway where he used the wall to steady himself and then up to the front door, which he opened.

There was a narrow, deteriorating set of three concrete steps down to an area that might have been all gravel at one time, but was now overgrown with dandelions and crabgrass. There was no railing for Shane to hold on to and he wasn't sure if his left knee had recovered enough to allow him to get down the steps, so he thought the safest thing to do was go down on his butt. He was about to sit down when he noticed to his left, an old, short-handled, wide mouth shovel leaning against the house beside the stairs. The blade was rusted and the shaft and handle were almost white with age, but Shane thought it looked sturdy. My new cane, Shane thought, as he reached over, picked up the shovel and pushed down on the handle to see if the blade would disintegrate if there was weight on it. Seems strong enough, he decided, held the handle in his right hand, put the shovel down next to the concrete steps, and used it to steady himself as he walked down.

Once he was at the bottom of the steps, Shane took in his surroundings while enjoying the fresh air. It was a sunny but chilly day, with only a few puffy clouds overhead, and the grass was still heavy with morning dew. Shane saw that he had been held captive in an old, narrow brick farmhouse and when he looked around the area he didn't see any buildings in the distance to indicate there were any neighbours nearby. There were two outbuildings on the property; a large implement shed and what remained of a barn, now just a field rock foundation surrounding a large pile of weathered boards.

There was no sign of a vehicle on the property, so using the shovel as a cane, Shane made his way over to the shed where he grabbed the handle on the tall, wide door and slid it open on its track. Inside, as Shane had only dared to hope, was his Charger.

He made his way with his makeshift support to the driver's door, which was unlocked, tossed the shove aside, got in, and was pleased to see that his cane was leaning against the passenger seat. The Charger started immediately, Shane backed it out of the shed, made a U-turn, and drove down the driveway, stopping at a gravel road. Which way? Shane asked himself. He leaned forward and looked up through the windshield and saw that while the sun was high in the sky, it wasn't directly overhead, but still to the east. There has to be neighbours around here where I can use a phone, Shane thought as he turned right and drove down the gravel road.

Chapter Twenty Two - Present

Emma had driven well above the speed limit from Logan Stewart's house to Burke and Associates downtown and was lucky enough to find a parking spot just up the street from the law firm.

After reading the text from Chioma while she sat in her vehicle in front of Logan's place, Emma had called right away and as soon as Chioma answered, she said excitedly, "It's Emma, what's happened!? Has Shane called? Is he okay?"

"Emma, there you are," Chioma replied with relief in her voice. "I got an email we think Shane sent. Can you come to the office?"

"I'm on my way," Emma said, disconnected the call, and started driving to King Street.

After parking, Emma walked quickly from her SUV, through the front door of the law firm, past receptionist Jill Langley without saying a word, and into Chioma's office where she saw the researcher at her desk working on a laptop and Jason Burke sitting beside her looking intently at the screen.

"Show me," was all Emma said as she walked around the desk.

"Hi, Emma, we have our fingers crossed," Jason said as he stood up to let Emma sit down beside Chioma.

Chioma turned the laptop slightly so Emma could see the screen better and after she read the contents of the email, Emma said excitedly, "It's got to be him! He used his middle name, 'Duke'. He hates that name because of his father and never, ever, mentions it to anyone."

"That's what I thought too," Jason said.

"Can you figure out where it came from, a location?" Emma asked Chioma.

"I've been trying, but I'm not having much luck," Chioma answered. "When I break it down into its code, the email was done in some type of encryption program that masked the IP address, and then it bounced around between servers in several countries before I got it. The bottom line is that it's virtually untraceable or at least well beyond my capabilities. So, Shane might have written the email, but he didn't send it."

"Jason, if this is Shane, why do you think that he, or more likely whoever kidnapped him, wants his notes from the Benson case?" Emma asked. "It has to be someone either connected to the Benson family or the murder victim, Paige Madison."

"We think Benson's son, Josh, is involved," Jason said. "We've had no luck trying to find him and neither have the police. Sergeant Lucas talked to Josh's mother, Alison, and she says she hasn't heard from Josh since he was medically discharged from the Canadian Forces."

"Why was he medically discharged?" Emma asked.

"Alison says Josh refused to tell her," Jason said. "I didn't tell Sergeant Lucas we already knew about the medical discharge because of how Chioma got the information. Last I heard, Lucas was making a formal request to the Canadian Forces for Josh's medical records."

"I bet Ben or Michelle can access them," Emma said.

"I didn't hear you say that for obvious reasons," Jason responded and then added, "If I did, I would tell you that if they got caught trying to hack into the Canadian Forces personnel records it would be a federal crime and they would go to jail for a very long time."

"Okay, getting back to the email, I assume you haven't told the police about it, as instructed," Emma said.

"We've thought about it," Jason said, "Because like in any other kidnapping case, it's the right thing to do, and they could bring in all of their resources."

Jason looked at Chioma who said, "But at this point, even with Shane's little known middle name, we're not sure if it's really from him. We thought we would answer first and see what happens. I was going to ask a question about his files that only Shane would know the answer to and see if we get a response."

"That's a great idea, let's do it," Emma said.

Chioma turned the laptop back to face her and started typing. After a few moments of work, she looked at Emma and Jason and said, "I've attached some of Shane's files from his computer, but I've told him he encrypted two of the more sensitive files and I need the key to access them. If it is him and he answers, only Shane would know one of the encryption keys we use in the office."

"Sounds good. Send it," Jason said and after Chioma did that, he said, "I guess now we wait."

The trio decided they would go to the staff lounge and have a coffee while they waited and Emma said she would tell them about her conversation with Logan Stewart. The lounge was a recent addition to Burke and Associates, an expansion of the old kitchenette into an unused office. It featured two small round tables with wooden chairs and there were several more comfortable chairs around the outside of the room. Along the counter with a sink, there was a microwave, a toaster and both a regular drip coffeemaker and a Keurig. It was a bright, people-friendly room that Jason said was his gift to the Associates and staff for their hard work and loyalty.

After they got their coffees, Emma, Jason and Chioma sat around one of the tables and Emma gave them the details of her visit to Logan Stewart's house, including how she lost her temper, which she wasn't sure she regretted anymore.

"You actually choked the guy?" Chioma asked, wondering about this side of Emma she didn't know existed.

"I lost it on him because I knew he was lying and with Shane missing, I didn't have time to play games with him," Emma said.

"With his mother as a witness, he could have you arrested and charged with assault," Jason said, his concern evident in his voice.

"There's little chance," Emma said. "Logan's looks and his demeanour told me he has a drug problem, likely crack, and I'm sure his poor mother knows too. The last thing she would want is Logan talking to the police."

"Do you think he knows something about Shane's disappearance?" Chioma asked.

"He's a liar which, unfortunately, is what many addicts become," Emma answered. "I plan to talk to Sergeant Lucas and convince him to have a hard look at Logan and hopefully get a warrant to search the basement of his mother's house where he lives."

While Emma was answering Chioma's question, Jason got quiet and very pensive. He had lost very few trials in his career and when he did, he took it very personally, none more than Gavin Benson's who he believed was wrongfully convicted and was confident he would have won on appeal if Gavin hadn't killed himself.

Emma saw that Jason had a look of concern on his face, so she asked, "What are you thinking, Jason?"

"I'm starting to wonder, based on what you've found out, if it was Logan who killed Paige and attended the trial to watch someone else take the blame," Jason said.

"That has occurred to me, Ben and Michelle," Emma said, but before she could continue, her phone started ringing. "Sorry, I better take this in case it's something important," she said as she took her phone out of her back pocket and walked out of the lounge and into the hallway.

Once she had left the room, Chioma said quietly to Jason, "I have no idea how she's keeping it together. I would be in pieces and unable to function if my husband or one of my kids went missing."

"She's a tough woman, maybe because of some of the things she saw when she was in the army and defusing landmines," Jason responded, also in a quiet voice. "But believe me, beneath that brave front that Emma is showing us, she's scared to death over the possibility that Shane is dead."

Suddenly, Jason and Chioma heard Emma cry out, "Oh my God, I don't believe it! I'm on my way!" and they looked at each other, both thinking the worst, that Shane's body had been found.

As they both got up from the table to go and comfort Emma, she appeared in the doorway and said, "Shane's at the Brantford Police Station!"

Chapter Twenty Three - The Trial

Crown Prosecutor Evan Gregory was about half an hour into his closing argument to the jury and Jason had to admit that his adversary was doing a very good job of arguing why Gavin Benson should be found guilty of second-degree murder.

Gregory would know, just as Jason did, that you run the risk of turning some of the jurors against you if you take too long with your final summation. The jurors had been sitting in a courtroom for over two weeks listening to hours of testimony and would be anxious to begin deliberation so they could make a decision and get back to their normal lives.

"Ladies and Gentlemen," Gregory said as he continued, "I'm quite sure that before you begin your deliberations, Judge Garnet, and most certainly my colleague Mr. Burke, will talk to you about the importance of being sure beyond a reasonable doubt when you find the defendant guilty. But I think you know the Crown has already done that."

"The proven facts in this case are clear: Gavin Benson took sexual advantage of a young woman under his supervision. He testified he and Paige Madison were in love and he planned to divorce his wife so they could be together. But he told his partner the affair was meaningless and he would end it or, in his own ominous words, 'take care of it', so we know Mr. Benson is a liar. He says he didn't know Paige was pregnant, but how are we supposed to believe that given all his other lies?

"The defendant admits he was with Paige the morning she was killed and the forensic evidence confirms they had sex, so we know he was with her and that shows opportunity. An expert testified the tire tracks near where Paige's body was found matched the tires that come standard with a Jeep Cherokee, the vehicle owned by the defendant."

Jason had fought hard to have the testimony about the tire tracks ruled inadmissible but lost and he still found Judge Garnet's ruling very puzzling. The Judge, well versed in common law, would know the scientific credibility of tire track evidence had been challenged many times and during his argument, Jason cited several examples in case law. He believed Garnet had made a serious mistake and if Gavin was found guilty, the Judge's decision would be the cornerstone of an appeal.

While Jason thought about the tire tracks, Gregory continued, "So, we have the opportunity and the means," he said, "That leaves motive and the defendant had plenty of that. He got caught having sex with a subordinate and it would mean the end of his marriage, probable alienation by his adult children, and as pointed out by his business partner, the possibility of a sexual harassment lawsuit. This would all come at a time when his business was in financial trouble."

"His psychiatrist testified Mr. Benson was suffering from depression and was taking mood-altering drugs. The thought of Paige ruining his life was too much. He decided she had to go, so after having sex with her one more time, he chokes her to death, abuses her body so it looks like she was attacked by a sexual sadist, and dumps her in a field."

"Motive, means and opportunity, all proven to you beyond a reasonable doubt. Your decision is clear; Gavin Benson is guilty of second-degree murder."

Gregory paused, scanned the faces of the jurors, and then said, "Ladies and Gentlemen, thank you for your service," before walking back to his desk, shaking hands with his associate, and sitting down.

"Thank you, Mr. Gregory. Mr. Burke, you may proceed with your closing argument," Judge Garnet said.

"Thank you, your Honour," Jason said as he got up from his chair and went and stood about halfway between his table and the railing in front of the jury, the prosecutor's table directly on his right. This position was on purpose; he wanted to be close to the jury, but not too close so they wouldn't feel he was trying to intimidate them, and he wanted the prosecutor close so that when he attacked the Crown's case, the jurors would only have to shift their eyes slightly to see Gregory's reaction.

"Members of the jury, I do not intend to be very long with my final argument because I'm confident that you already know my colleague,

Mr. Gregory, is wrong when he says there's no reasonable doubt in this case. The fact is, it's riddled with it."

"Let's start with the forensic evidence. There isn't any, other than my client's DNA matching the semen found in Paige Madison's body, which was expected because Gavin says he had sex with Paige the morning of the day she was killed. But that's it. Nothing else was found on Paige's body that linked Gavin to her murder. She was choked to death, but you didn't hear the pathologist say there was evidence found on her neck that could identify her killer other than she believed it was a right-handed male. The wooden handles used to penetrate Paige were not found, so no fingerprints."

"Then there's the big deal the prosecutor is making about the tire treads found near Paige's body, supposedly the type common to Jeep Cherokees. You didn't hear the expert say they were an exact match to the Jeep driven by my client because the tread marks were too muddy to make that kind of comparison. So what does that leave? Tires common to a very popular vehicle of which there are thousands in the area. I think it's a safe bet there are people in this courtroom right now, maybe one of you on the jury, who owned a Jeep Cherokee at the time of the murder. My wife did, so maybe she should have been questioned by the police."

Jason's remark caused a bit of a stir, including a few chuckles from observers in the courtroom, which drew a scowl from Judge Garnet, and put a smile on members of the jury.

"And one more important thing about the lack of forensic evidence," Jason said. "Forensic experts went over my client's vehicle with a fine tooth comb and did not find one shred of evidence that Paige had ever been in it. You will note that the prosecutor didn't mention that fact during the presentation of the Crown's case."

After pausing to let the jury consider what he had said so far, Jason continued, "And now, let's consider the crux of the Crown's case, motive," he said. "But before I do that, there's something else that I can't leave unchallenged. During Doctor Jacob's testimony, Mr. Gregory tried desperately to get the psychiatrist to agree that the anti-depressants he prescribed my client could possibly have turned Gavin into a completely different person, an aggressive individual capable of violence. I didn't counter this with expert testimony because I was confident you already knew it was a ridiculous theory. You'll notice the prosecutor didn't put an expert on the stand to say anti-depressants caused violent behaviour because he knew such cases were extremely rare."

"During his summation, the Prosecutor again alluded to mood-altering drugs. The use of different types of anti-depressants is widespread in this country and I guarantee you there are people in this courtroom today, perhaps including several of you on the jury, who are taking medications to successfully deal with depression and anxiety. It's thought that anti-depressants work by increasing levels of chemicals in your brain called neurotransmitters and some of them, like serotonin and noradrenaline, are linked to mood and emotion. But ask yourself. How people do you know who are taking anti-depressants have become angry and violent?"

Jason again paused briefly, then continued, "And now, motive. You will have to decide on the credibility of the people who testified during this trial in order to determine, beyond a reasonable doubt, that Gavin Benson had the motive to kill Paige. During their separate testimonies, Gavin and his partner, Ethan Holdaway, strongly disagreed about some of the things they said to each other when they discussed Gavin's affair with Paige. So who are you supposed to believe? Holdaway claims Gavin was very angry when he said, 'Don't worry, I'll take care of it. She won't be a problem'. Holdaway says he was very concerned about what Gavin would do. Well, you saw my client's instantaneous reaction when he stood up in this courtroom and vehemently denied that was how the conversation went. So who's telling the truth? If you're not sure, that's reasonable doubt."

"And what about the testimony of Paige's friend, Ariel Durst? She admitted that even though she had never met my client, she resented him for getting involved with Paige and eventually that resentment turned to hate. She claims she didn't embellish what Paige told her, but how can we be sure she's telling the truth if she hated Gavin and had already decided he was guilty? It raises reasonable doubt."

"And finally, my client's side of the story. Gavin was in love with Paige and says she felt the same way. He was happy for the first time in years and was prepared to end his marriage to be with Paige. He didn't know she was pregnant but says if she told him, he would have been elated. Gavin understood his partner's concerns about the legal and financial implications if his relationship with Paige ended badly, but he says it was never going to happen because of how they felt about each other. And he says Ethan was making a big deal out of it to distance himself from any possible fallout and to deflect from the fact that he was responsible for much of the company's current financial problems."

"So, who do you believe?" Jason asked. "Well, I would suggest it doesn't matter because if you're not absolutely sure in the first place, that's reasonable doubt and you can't convict."

Jason took a couple of steps toward the jury to add some intimacy to his conclusion.

"Ladies and Gentlemen," he said. "I would ask you to put aside any opinion you might have about December-May relationships. A large gap in ages between lovers is more common than you think. There's a fifteen year difference in ages between my wife and me, and we've been happily married for over twenty five years. My wife's parents got married when her mother was seventeen and he was thirty."

"Gavin Benson and Paige Madison didn't care about the difference in their ages because they were in love. Gavin didn't kill Paige, he wanted to be with her. And the Crown has failed to prove beyond a reasonable doubt that he was responsible for her death."

Jason returned to his table and sat down, and felt the adrenaline that had coursed through his body during his final argument dissipate, leaving behind an exhaustion compounded by the fact the trial would soon be in the hands of the jury. Gavin sat stoically beside him and Jason could see that he was deep in thought and probably fighting the anxiety over what the jury would decide.

Judge Garnet began his charge to the jury in which he would, among other things, outline in understandable terms the law the jurors must apply when they're assessing the facts they believe to be true.

As the Judge talked, Jason again studied the jury, hoping to get some sense of what they were thinking, but they remained a mystery to him. This was the first time he could remember reaching the end of a trial and not having extensive notes on every juror and how he believed they were leaning; for or against the defence. The entire jury didn't feel right to him and he was starting to think he had failed during the jury selection to make sure there was a balanced panel.

It was mid-afternoon by the time Judge Garnet completed his charge and sent the jury out to begin deliberations. After changing out of his court robe and white tabs and into a regular suit jacket, Jason went with Gavin to a holding cell in the basement of the courthouse to wait and was pleased to see the court officer had put two comfortable chairs in the cell for them to use. The officer brought them coffee and told Jason that if the jury was still out, he would bring him a meal when it was time for Gavin to eat.

Gavin was silent for a long time and Jason left him to his thoughts and instead worked his way through the emails on his phone, deleting some and answering those that needed immediate attention. He had to stop working the keyboard with his thumbs several times to review what he had typed, his mind distracted by his inability to read the mood of the jury.

Was it possible he didn't want to admit to himself that he had failed to convince even one of them there was enough reasonable doubt to find Gavin not guilty? He realized that he had been ignoring the fact that one of the jurors, a middle-aged woman with two teenage daughters, had constantly stolen glances at Gavin, and not in a good way. Was it disgust he was seeing in her face?

After taking a lot longer than normal to answer a text message because his mind was still focused on the trial, Jason heard Gavin clear his throat and when he looked up from his phone at him, his client spoke for the first time since they arrived in the holding cell.

"Do you think they believed me, that I didn't kill Paige?" Gavin asked softly and though he may have had trouble reading the faces of the jurors, Jason had no problem recognizing the fear in Benson's eyes.

"To be honest, I don't know," Jason answered, but then quickly added, "But I do know that you did very well on the stand and came across as very credible and genuine in your feelings about Paige."

Gavin went silent again, looked away from Jason, and stared blankly at the holding cell wall. Jason returned his attention to his phone, but after a few moments, Gavin said to him, "You don't have to wait with me, Jason, I'll be fine, and I'm sure you'd like to get home and see your wife. Really, I'm okay to wait by myself."

"I don't mind waiting in case there's an early verdict or until the jury decides to quit for the day and start again tomorrow," Jason said.

"I appreciate that and I appreciate how hard you've worked for me," Gavin said, "But go home. I think I would prefer some time by myself anyway."

"Okay, Gavin, if that's what you would like," Jason said as he stood and put his phone in the inner pocket of his suit coat. His large file case on wheels with a long handle for pulling, like a piece of luggage, was near the open door of the cell. As he was leaving with it, Jason turned and said to Gavin, "If you need me for any reason, the officer on duty will know how to contact me."

As it turned out, the jury didn't reach a decision that day and was sequestered for the night at a nearby motel. Jason got a call in his office shortly after eleven the next morning informing him the jury had reached a verdict and court would resume at 1 pm.

Jason was in the courtroom by 12:30 and it was already jammed with spectators as word a verdict had been reached spread quickly. Paige's parents, Anna and Bill, were there, surrounded by other family members. Jason saw that the Madison's were holding hands and they both looked haggard from the ordeal they had been through.

Gavin's wife, Alison, was noticeably absent but his daughter Melissa and his son Josh, wearing his Armed Forces dress uniform, were seated a couple of rows behind the defence table.

Ariel Durst was there with, Jason assumed, several of her and Paige's mutual friends. Some of the usual trial junkies had managed to find a seat and Jason noted the red curly-haired young man who had attended every day of the trial.

His investigator, Shane Daniels, was sitting on the bench directly behind him and smiled at Jason as a sign of encouragement. Shane had put in a lot of hours investigating the case and Jason knew Shane was disappointed he didn't find anything substantial that could be used to put forward an alternate suspect in Paige's murder.

At exactly the scheduled time, Judge Garnet entered the courtroom and everyone stood until he took his seat on the dais. The Clerk called the case, Regina vs Benson, and the Judge asked that the jury be brought in.

The jurors all kept their faces expressionless as they filed in and took their seats, but Jason noticed that several did take a quick glance at Gavin as they sat down.

Judge Garnet made a few remarks about decorum in the courtroom after the verdict was read and warned that outbursts would not be tolerated. He then turned to the jury and one specific individual; a big, tall man Jason knew was in his sixties and owned several gas bars in the city.

Jason instructed Gavin to stand up beside him, which he did.

"Mr. Foreperson, has the jury reached a unanimous verdict in the charge of second-degree murder against the defendant Gavin Benson?" Garnet asked.

"We have your Honour," the man stood up and said. "We, the jury, find Gavin Benson guilty."

A rumble of voices rolled across the gallery and Jason heard a few gasps. Gavin started to collapse beside him, so Jason grabbed him by the arm to hold him up.

"This is not over yet, Gavin, do you hear me?" Jason said into Benson's ear. "I told you there are a lot of grounds for appeal if we lost and I meant that. You have to stay strong. Do you understand?" Gavin nodded his head slowly and steadied himself. People in the courtroom were still reacting to the verdict and Judge Garnet banged his gavel several times to restore order.

Suddenly, Jason heard someone behind him yell, "This is bullshit and you know it!" Jason turned and saw it was Gavin's son, Josh, who then stormed out of the courtroom, his sister, Melissa, not far behind.

Another bang from Garnet's gavel and the courtroom became silent. Jason whispered to Gavin that they should remain standing because the Judge would ask for that anyway. Jason removed his hand from Gavin's arm, hoping his client could keep his composure.

"Mr. Burke, do you wish to have a poll of the jury?" Garnet asked. Under the law, Jason had the right to have each juror stand and state they agreed with the second-degree murder verdict that came with an automatic life sentence.

"No, your Honour," Jason replied.

"Very well," Garnet responded and then turning his attention to Gavin, said, "Mr. Benson, you have been found guilty of second-degree murder which carries an automatic sentence of twenty five years. The only decision that remains is when you might be eligible for parole, the earliest being ten years. I am ordering a pre-sentence report and you will be returned to this courtroom in four weeks to hear my decision. This court is adjourned."

Judge Garnet stood, everyone else did the same, and he left by a side door. While the spectators started to file out of the courtroom, an officer came to the defence table to take Gavin into custody.

"Remember what I told you," Jason said to Gavin, whose face had gone ashen and he looked like he had aged ten years.

After Gavin left with the officer, Jason started gathering up his files and notes and putting them in his carrier. Shane, who had stayed as the courtroom emptied, leaned over the waist high railing and said, "I'm sorry, Jason, I thought you did more than enough to raise reasonable doubt. I didn't think the jury would ever come up with a unanimous decision and at a minimum, you'd get a new trial."

"Thanks, Shane," Jason said as he continued to put files in his carrier. "I admit I never really got a handle on how the jurors were leaning. But, the grounds for an appeal are strong and I'll get started on that right away."

"I keep thinking I missed something. I need to start over," Shane said.

"That's fine, I appreciate that I really do," Jason said and then added, "But we also have to move on. I have several other cases sitting on my desk and with some of them, I'm going to need your undivided attention."

"Are you going to be alright? You want to go grab a coffee or something?" Shane asked.

He knew that his brilliant lawyer friend, who lost very few cases, would be taking the guilty verdict hard and would be blaming himself.

"Thanks, but I have a few things to deal with in terms of Gavin's transfer to a permanent jail cell and I want to check on him," Jason said.

"He took it hard," Shane stated.

"Yeah, I'm worried about his mental state. I need to keep reminding him we have excellent grounds for an appeal," Jason said.

After Shane left and he had completed gathering his files, Jason walked over to the prosecution table where Evan Gregory was doing the same thing. They shook hands and exchanged a few words, nothing specific about the case, and Jason returned to his table to get his wheeled file carrier.

He was tired and deeply disappointed with the jury's verdict. I just don't understand how they could reach a unanimous decision when there was so little evidence that directly linked Gavin to the murder, he thought.

Every member of the jury must have been convinced that Gavin was lying about the nature of his relationship with Paige and that he wanted her out of the way before she caused him personal and financial problems. But I'll never know what they were thinking.

Unlike in the United States, jurors in Canada are forbidden by law to publicly discuss their deliberations and the reasons for their verdict.

The law had been changed to allow jurors to discuss the case with mental health professionals if they were struggling with what they heard during a trial.

I need to clear my head of the emotions I'm feeling right now about what happened in this courtroom, Jason thought, and get down to the business of overturning the verdict.

Chapter Twenty Four - Present

Emma was so excited about the news that Shane was alive and safe that she almost didn't stop at the reception desk at the Brantford Police Service headquarters on Elgin Street.

After entering the front door, she started walking directly to the door to the left of reception, which she knew led to the Detective's Division, caught herself, asked the woman behind the counter for Sergeant Lucas, and then paced back and both while she waited.

Lucas appeared at the security door with a big smile on his face and Emma stepped quickly to follow him into the extensive administration and office area. They walked down a hallway with an open area to the left and offices on the right, stopping at the closed door of an interview room. Emma could see Shane through the window of the door, sitting at a table with a uniformed officer across from him. Lucas used his security card to unlock the door and as Emma rushed in, Shane jumped up from his chair and they embraced.

"Oh, Shane, thank God! I never gave up hope you were alive!" Emma cried, tears of joy running down her face.

"I'm okay, Emma. I'm so sorry this happened," Shane said as tears also ran down his face. "I must smell pretty bad," he added.

"Yes, you do," Emma responded. They both chuckled as they stood holding on tight to each other and Emma said, "But at this point, that's the last thing I care about."

Lucas, who was standing at the open door, said, "We're going to give you a few minutes alone, but then we'll need time with Shane to get his statement. Emma, paramedics checked Shane over and he's physically fine. They did give him something for his knee, which he was having trouble with. If you want to wait until we're finished, we'll find you a comfortable spot."

The other officer in the room got up and left with Lucas, who pulled the door closed. Shane got the chair on the other side of the table so he and Emma could sit facing each other and hold hands.

"I tried to hold it together, but I was sick with fear over the thought I had lost you," Emma said emotionally. "You can tell me the whole story when I get you home, but what happened? Where were you!?"

Shane said that he was drugged and taken captive by Josh Benson who locked him in a sealed room Josh had prepared in advance. Josh gave him the trial transcripts and threatened to kill him unless Shane could prove his father was wrongfully convicted by figuring out who actually murdered Paige Madison.

"He expected you to solve an already solved murder while locked in a room and with just a trial transcript?" Emma wondered.

Shane explained that Josh told him he was dying from an inoperable brain tumour and how he believed that played a major role in affecting Josh's actions.

"I managed to escape from the room Josh was holding me in, I'll tell you how later, and drive away in the Charger," Shane continued. "I followed a gravel road until I came to Highway 52, realized I was somewhere in the Ancaster area, and drove here. After I explained the situation, Brantford cops contacted the OPP, who patrol the area where I was held and, as far as I know, officers went to the farmhouse and arrested Josh, who I left locked in the room when I escaped."

"While we were desperately trying to find you, Jason, Ben, Michelle and I believed that Josh was a primary suspect in your disappearance," Emma said.

"Ben and Michelle came down from Port Elgin to help you?" Shane asked.

"They didn't hesitate, they just showed up," Emma said.

"Is Ben driving you crazy with his inappropriate comments and probably trying unsuccessfully not to swear in front of Lan?" Shane asked with a smile on his face.

"No comment on that," Emma replied, smiling back. "But he and Michelle have been a big help and I've really appreciated their support."

"I love you, Emma. I was afraid I would never see you and Lan again," Shane said softly as he put his hand on the side of Emma's face.

Emma leaned forward and they kissed. "I want you home as soon as possible, so I'll go, you tell Lucas everything he wants to know for now, and then we can get out of here," Emma said.

"A hot shower and some decent food sounds really good to me," Shane said.

"And some time alone with me?" Emma asked.

"Definitely some time alone with you," Shane said.

His statement and answering questions about what happened took over two hours and when it reached that length, Shane said he'd had enough and wanted to go home. Lucas told him that Josh was in custody and being interrogated, but was being uncooperative, saying he wouldn't talk to the police who conspired to convict his father of murder and were responsible for his suicide. Shane told Lucas that Josh was sick and needed help.

After saying there would be follow-up questions and a meeting with someone from the Crown Attorney's office, Lucas let Shane leave with Emma, who had waited the entire time in a comfortable chair in the small reception area outside of the Police Chief's office. Already briefed on the situation, Chief Charlie Oak came out of his office with two mugs of coffee and sat with Emma for over half an hour. Oak was his training officer during Shane's brief time with the

Brantford Police Service and was with him at the domestic disturbance call where a drunken man shot Shane in the knee with a shotgun. The man had already fired at Oak, who was saved by his bulletproof vest, and Shane was hit as he pushed the man's equally inebriated wife out of the line of fire. Shane then shot and killed the assailant.

While Oak rose through the ranks to eventually become Chief, he and Shane remained friends. Oak was particularly supportive when Shane had to leave the police service on disability and struggled with depression, booze and pills.

The Chief told Emma that he had received a briefing every day when Shane was missing and made sure the search for him remained active. Emma liked Oak because of everything he did for Shane, but only half believed what he told her because she was convinced the officers working Shane's case had given up looking for him and were just waiting for his body to show up.

When Shane and Emma finally got home it was late afternoon and as soon as they walked through the front door, Lan came running out of her room, Shane knelt and they hugged. Emma had called Ben and Michelle from the police station and asked them to meet Lan's bus when she came home from school.

"You're going to hug the air out of my lungs, little Miss Lan," Shane teased.

"I knew you weren't dead, Shane!" Lan exclaimed. "Nobody wanted to talk about it when I was around, but I knew you were coming home because you promised we would watch 'Avatar: The Last Airbender' together, remember?"

"I remember," Shane said. "I thought about my promise a lot when I was away and couldn't get home."

While Shane and Lan were hugging, Ben and Michelle walked out of the kitchen, both with big smiles on their faces. They took turns embracing Shane.

"Fuck, man, you scared the shit out of us," Ben said.

"Ben…," Emma started.

"Sorry, I forgot again," Ben said sheepishly and Lan giggled.

"Thanks, you guys, for coming and helping Emma, and being here for her," Shane said to Ben and Michelle.

"You would do the same for me and you have in the past," Ben said and then looked at Emma and said proudly, "Did you notice? Not one F-bomb in that sentence."

"You're a real hero," Emma said sarcastically and Lan started giggling again.

Shane went and shaved, he had several days of heavy growth to deal with, had a long, hot shower and put on fresh clothes. He looked at the floor of the bedroom where he had piled the jeans, golf shirt, underwear and socks that he had on during his captivity and decided he was going to throw them out so they wouldn't be around as a reminder of what he went through.

Emma ordered a lot of Chinese food and when it arrived, she opened all of the containers on the kitchen table and everyone helped themselves. "This is way better than the slop on my buffet that I feed the tourists," Ben remarked.

"Don't listen to him," Shane said to Lan while she was filling her plate. "Ben's restaurant is very popular and his food is excellent."

"You have to say that because you're my friend," Ben responded and then smiled at Emma in case she didn't notice he had again avoided saying fuck.

After dinner, Lan went to her room to look at her tablet and Shane gave Emma, Ben and Michelle a detailed explanation of what happened to him and answered all of their questions. Ben and Michelle decided that since it wasn't too late, they were going to go and check out of their motel and then drive home to Port Elgin.

Later that night, after making love and lying in each other's arms for a long time, Emma drifted off to sleep but even though he was physically exhausted, Shane was still wide awake. His time in captivity was haunting him and he felt like he was having a nightmare even though he wasn't asleep. He could still hear the ear-piercing loud music and feel the burn of the bright lights on his eyelids. Am I in shock? Shane asked himself. Is this how it felt?

Unable to take it anymore, Shane sat up in bed with the intention of going to the kitchen, making some tea, and sitting at the table to see if he could clear his head. Emma stirred beside him and he heard her whisper, "What's the matter? Are you okay?"

"I'm having some trouble processing what happened. It's like it's on a tape loop, playing over and over in my head," Shane whispered back. "I'm sorry if I woke you. Go back to sleep, I'm going to get up for a while."

"There's no way you're sitting up alone," Emma said as she threw back her covers and reached down to the floor to get her prosthetic leg. "I'll make some coffee or tea, whatever you would prefer."

Shane and Emma ended up spending two hours sitting at the kitchen table, drinking tea, and talking, which Shane did most of.

"Maybe you should talk to someone about what you went through, maybe Charlene," Emma said at one point. Charlene Anderson was a psychiatrist and Emma's friend, and it was through her that Emma did her volunteer counselling with recent amputees.

"I'll think about it," was all Shane said.

At mid-morning the next day, after finally getting some sleep, Shane awoke suddenly from a vivid dream and it took a few moments for him to get his bearings, to realize he was in his bed at home.

In the dream, Shane was back sitting on the floor of the basement room where he was held captive, but everything around him was fuzzy and indistinct. Loud heavy metal music was playing and Shane was bobbing his head in enjoyment while he tossed pages from the Benson trial up in the air. Paige Madison was there, her long blonde hair was a tangled mess and Shane could see dirt and blades of grass in it. Paige was moving slowly and seductively to the music, running her hands over her breasts under a torn and soiled blouse.

"You're a tease," Shane said in his dream.

"I don't care. You're too young for me," Paige said.

Normally, like a lot of people, Shane would wake up knowing he just had a vivid dream, but couldn't remember what the dream was about. He always assumed our brain wiped out our memory of most dreams so we didn't go insane because we weren't sure what was reality and what was not.

But the details of this dream stayed with him and when Shane thought about it, he realized his subconscious had reminded him about something he read in the Benson trial transcript that he had wondered about and could be a possible clue to Paige's real killer.

Chapter Twenty Five - Present

Shane spent two days at home before returning to work at Burke and Associates, some of it staring mindlessly at the TV, but most of it reading through his files on the Benson case, which he accessed remotely from the computer in his office.

He was called back to the Brantford Police station to put the final touches on, and then sign, his official statement on his kidnapping and while he was there, Sergeant Lucas told him that Josh Benson had been ordered to undergo both a complete medical exam and a psychiatric evaluation. Lucas said that Josh's mother had hired a lawyer who was already indicating that Josh would be pleading not criminally responsible for the charges against him because of mental disorder. The Sergeant figured that Josh would likely have a strong argument given the brain tumour he had.

Shane also agreed to go with one of the Detectives assigned to the case and an Assistant Crown Attorney back to the Ancaster area farmhouse where he was held. The house, it turned out, was owned by one of Josh's friends in the Canadian Forces who agreed to let Josh stay there and it was why no one, including his mother, knew where Josh was after he was discharged from the army.

When they arrived at the isolated farmhouse, Shane saw police tape strung around the front door and an OPP cruiser in the driveway, an officer there to keep the scene secure until all of the forensics had been collected.

It was difficult for Shane to be back in the basement room where he was drugged, tortured with light and sound, and believed he was going to die. The Detective, pretending he was Josh, asked Shane to demonstrate how he overpowered the former soldier and his actions after he escaped. The Assistant Crown Attorney asked a lot of questions about Shane's time in captivity and what Josh demanded of him. Shane was getting tired of repeating his story over and over, his patience wearing thin because he wanted to forget what happened and not keep reliving it.

When Shane walked into the law firm after the two days at home, Jill Langley came out from behind the reception desk and hugged him.

"Everyone was so worried about you," Jill said. "I'm so happy you're safe and sound."

"Thanks, Jill, I appreciate that," Shane said and started toward his office, but he didn't get far before he was surrounded by the firm's Associates and Law Clerks who wanted to welcome him back. Shane spent fifteen minutes talking with everyone and answering their questions before resuming the walk to his office.

Jill still liked to handle telephone messages the old-fashioned way with handwritten pink paper slips, so Shane sat at his desk and sorted through the pile of slips on his desk; important ones on the left and those that could wait on the right.

When he was off, Shane bought a new phone and after retrieving them from the cloud, went through the dozens of emails and texts he had received while he was held captive in the basement room. He knew he could also retrieve voice messages left on his old phone, but he decided against it because he knew there would be messages from Emma desperately trying to get in touch with him. It would hurt too much to listen to them, so he just deleted the files.

There were a lot of things Shane had to get caught up on, but he was anxious to talk to Jason, so he left all of that behind and walked down the row of offices to the large corner one. The door was open and Jason was sitting sideways behind his large, beautiful mahogany desk, facing a sideboard that held the keyboard and wide-screen monitor for his computer.

Shane knocked on the door and when he walked in, Jason looked up from what he was doing, smiled and said, "Welcome back! Come on in."

Jason, as usual, was in a tailored suit, the jacket over the back of his chair. He was wearing a very light blue dress shirt, a red silk tie and gold cuff links. There were two comfortable metal framed, padded leather chairs facing the desk and as soon as Shane sat down, Jason asked, "How are you? You could have taken as much time as you needed."

"I'm fine," Shane said and then added, "I'm ready to put the whole thing behind me, but not quite yet."

"What do you mean, not quite yet?" Jason asked.

"You know how you always say that mistakes in a case are often linked to questions you should've asked but didn't? I think there were some important questions I failed to ask while investigating Paige Madison's murder and the case against Gavin Benson," Shane said.

"Okay, but be honest with me," Jason said, "Are you also saying there were important questions I failed to ask witnesses during the trial? Questions that might have raised even more reasonable doubt than I managed to do or perhaps could have proven Benson was innocent?"

"I think there were questions you could have asked if I had done a better job getting them for you," Shane answered.

"Like what? What are you thinking was missed?" Jason asked.

"I think the key to the whole thing starts with Paige," Shane responded. "What if she wasn't exactly the beautiful, innocent young woman with the heart of gold that everyone made her out to be? When I was in captivity and forced to read the trial transcripts, I kept coming back to, and even made a note, about something Gavin's partner Ethan Holdaway said about Paige during your cross-examination. He called her a flirt around the men in the office and suggested she was doing that to help advance her position in the company. But, he claimed she never flirted with him, which is strange since he was one of the owners of the company."

"You think he lied about that?" Jason asked.

"Let me tell you something first," Shane replied. "When I was off the past two days, I realized I didn't do nearly enough background on the victim, so I started poking around in Paige's life and found one of the mistakes I made. When I was online looking up the address where she lived, there was a real estate ad about an available apartment in her building. I already knew it was a high-end building, but I was surprised that they wanted twenty two hundred a month plus utilities. There's no way an administrative assistant making, at most, maybe thirty five thousand a year could afford that. And when I checked, at the time of her death Paige was driving a 2023 Rav4. So, she was living in an expensive apartment, likely had a hefty car loan, and probably still had a student loan to pay."

"Maybe her parents were helping her out," Jason remarked.

"I highly doubt they could help that much," Shane said. "Her father is a lower middle-income earner and her mother only works part-time. It's a safe bet someone else was helping Paige financially. Did Gavin ever say anything about giving her money?"

"Not that I recall," Jason answered. "The Crown subpoenaed his and the business's financial records prior to the trial and I remember reviewing them to see what they might be after, but I don't remember any unusual payments that stood out. I could have Chioma take another look."

"I would appreciate that," Shane said. "I need to know if Gavin was propping her up financially and if so, when did he start. Also, during the trial, both you and Gregory asked a lot of questions regarding the financial state of Grand River Associates, but what about Ethan Holdaway's financial records?"

"Yes, they were there," Jason answered. "I had them reviewed in case there was something I could use to help discredit his testimony, but there was no 'smoking gun' as they say."

"We need to take another look," Shane said.

"What are you thinking, Shane?" Jason asked.

"What if I'm right and Paige wasn't so sweet and innocent? She told her friend Ariel Durst she wasn't interested in guys her own age and was attracted to older men. Maybe that was because older men meant financial security for her, a beautiful apartment, a new car and nice clothes. What if she had that kind of relationship going on in secret, but it ended, so she hooked up with Gavin. Or maybe she legitimately fell in love with Gavin, who could also look after her financial needs, which she would have considered a bonus, so she dumped her current provider. He didn't take it too well when he found out about Gavin, he got angry and killed her."

"So you no longer consider Josh Benson or Logan Stewart, Paige's stalker, as viable suspects?" Jason asked.

"They're not ruled out just yet," Shane answered. "But I'm convinced the theory I gave you is the right one."

"If Paige had something going with another older man before Gavin, you think it's possible it was Ethan Holdaway?" Jason said, sounding skeptical.

"I do," Shane said. "I just have to prove it."

Chapter Twenty Six - Present

Edna Montour, the receptionist at Grand River Associates, was a short, overweight woman and Shane estimated she was in her early sixties. He knew she was a member of the Six Nations and lived with her husband on the reserve, south of Brantford, near the village of Ohsweken.

It was just after 5 pm and Shane was sitting in the Charger, parked across the street from the business, watching as employees walked out the door, their work day over. There were substantially fewer people employed at Grand River compared to well over a year ago when Gavin Benson was charged with Paige Madison's murder. The engineering firm was already faltering at that time and there were serious doubts it would survive after Benson was found guilty, but somehow Ethan Holdaway was keeping the doors open.

Shane watched as Holdaway left the building and walked purposely down the sidewalk, likely headed for the municipal parking garage less than two blocks away. Edna was last to leave, so she locked the heavy glass door and pulled on the handle a couple of times to ensure the deadbolt had engaged. She then turned and started walking in the opposite direction of Holdaway. Shane got out of the Charger and watched as Edna walked toward a small municipal parking lot. He crossed the street and followed, catching up with her just as she was approaching a white Ford Escape SUV.

"Excuse me, Edna," Shane said before he got too close, so he didn't startle the woman.

Edna turned and looked at Shane, her face a mix of both curiosity and concern over being approached by a stranger when there were no other people around.

Shane stopped at least four feet away and said, "Edna, hi, I don't know if you remember me or not, but I'm Shane Daniels. I work with Jason Burke, the lawyer who represented Gavin Benson at his trial. You and I met when I came by the office to talk to you about a week after Paige Madison's body was found."

"You look vaguely familiar, but I can't say I remember talking to you," Edna said in a cautious voice. "I was interviewed by several people around that time. What can I do for you? I'm heading home for the day, but I'll be back in the office tomorrow."

"To be honest, I wanted to talk to you outside of the office," Shane said, keeping his voice even so Edna didn't think he was being aggressive or perhaps threatening. "Can we walk someplace and talk? Maybe have a coffee?" Shane asked.

"No, I would like to get home," Edna replied firmly and then asked, "What is it you want, Mr. Daniels, that can't wait until I'm in the office tomorrow?"

Shane reached into the inside pocket of the light jacket he was wearing and removed several sheets of paper that were stapled together and folded in half. He stepped up and stood beside Edna, unfolded the papers, and held them out so she could see what was on them.

"Edna, it turned out you didn't have to testify at the Benson trial because the prosecution and the defence mutually agreed to the admission of this," Shane said as he pointed to the papers he was showing, "It's a paper copy of the appointment calendar you had on your computer the day Paige was murdered. You used the calendar program to keep track of who's in and out of the office."

"Why are you asking me about this now?" Edna asked, her growing irritation evident in her voice.

"I have an important question about it that you would know the answer to," Shane said. "It says on the day Paige was murdered, Gavin Benson didn't arrive at the office until 10:20 am. You noted another employee leaving at 11:15 for a medical appointment and two leaving at 11:55 for lunch. Then, at 1 pm, it says 'Ethan Holdaway out' and nothing else, which is strange because I can see you keep meticulous records, always noting where people are going. How come you didn't note where Mr. Holdaway was going?"

"I don't know, I guess I forgot to ask him where he was going when he left. I don't remember. That was well over a year ago," Edna said defensively. "You'll have to ask him."

"I plan to," Shane said. "But, Edna, I have no doubt this would have been one of the most memorable days in your life. Our receptionist knows about everything that goes on in our office, so I think it's a safe bet you were aware of the big argument that took place between Mr. Benson and Mr. Holdaway about Paige. Then, the next day, you find out she was murdered. I think you do know where Mr. Holdaway was going when he left the office the day she was killed."

"I said I don't remember. It might have been to see a client," Edna said and then reached into her purse and took out her keys. "I have to go," she said and turned toward her car.

"Edna, I don't think you're being honest with me," Shane said firmly.

"I don't have to answer your questions!" Edna said angrily. "You're harassing me for no reason! That whole sad affair is in the past. Gavin killed Paige. Now let me go!

"Okay, Edna, that's fine," Shane responded and then said, "But I have a lot of friends at Brantford Police, as does my boss, Jason Burke, so I will be coming to see you again, but the next time it will be an official police interview and not a friendly chat like today."

Shane was bluffing. In fact, the entire conversation was a shot in the dark as he tried to prove the theory he had about Paige's murder. But then, to his surprise, his bluff worked.

"I don't want to get in trouble," Edna said as she turned back from her car to face Shane, who saw worry in her face.

"You won't be in trouble, Edna," Shane said. "What did Mr. Holdaway say that day when he left the office?"

"He walked by my desk on the way out the door without saying anything, so I asked him where he was going and what time he thought he would be back in case a client called for him," Agnes explained. "He asked me to do him a favour and not put anything on the log and he'd be back in a couple of hours. He must have seen the look on my face because he knows how fussy I am about the calendar. He said it wasn't a big deal, that his wife was having a problem with her vehicle and he needed to take it to the dealer to get fixed because she needed to use it."

"But you went ahead and marked him as out anyway," Shane said.

"I couldn't help myself," Edna said and Shane realized she probably had the kind of obsessive-compulsive disorder where everything has to be orderly and balanced, and that was why her records were so meticulous.

"Do you happen to know what kind of vehicle Mrs. Holdaway drives?" Shane asked.

"Well, she's got a new car now, but I remember at the time she was driving a Jeep of some kind," Edna answered.

After thanking Edna for her honesty and telling her again that she was not in trouble, Shane returned to where he parked the Charger. When he got inside, he looked up the street at the parking lot and saw that Edna was still standing beside her car, staring at the pavement, deep in thought. She's realized what she told me could mean, Shane said to himself.

Chapter Twenty Seven - Present

Emma looked at her image in the mirror on the back of the sun visor in her SUV and chuckled to herself when she thought about what Shane asked her to do.

"I need a beautiful woman with lots of feminine charm who's also a good actress," Shane said to her. "That would be you."

While Emma appreciated the compliments, she wasn't sure if Shane was seeing the same woman she was looking at in the mirror. Although they had faded somewhat since his return, Emma could still see dark circles under her eyes from the lack of sleep and the stress she was under during Shane's disappearance and she figured the deeper worry lines beside her eyes and lips were there to stay.

Emma took the compact out of her purse and applied makeup to cover up the dark circles and then put on some lipstick. That's going to have to do, she thought, as she closed the mirror and put the visor back in place.

There were two Dodge Chrysler dealerships in the city, but the one Emma was parked at on Lyndon Road dealt exclusively with Jeep products. She took a deep breath to calm her nerves, got out of her SUV, and entered the door to the Service Department.

The reception area was bright and clean with comfortable looking chairs and even a sofa for customers waiting for their vehicles to be serviced. Emma walked to the counter where a young man was looking at a large computer monitor and working on the keyboard. She figured he was in his mid to late twenties and the badge on his uniform shirt said he was Steve, a Service Consultant. Steve wasn't tall, but he was a big man, more overweight than muscular. He had dark hair and a day's growth of beard, a flat, broad nose, a developing double chin and a deeply pitted complexion suggesting a teenage battle with severe acne.

When Steve noticed Emma at the counter, he stepped away from the computer, faced her, and said, "Hi! How can I help you?"

"Hi yourself, Steve. I'm Emma," Emma said with a smile.

"What can I do for you, Emma?" Steve said.

"I need a bit of a favour, Steve," Emma began. "I'm a single woman who, quite frankly, doesn't know anything about cars other than how to drive them. But I have the opportunity to buy a 2023 Jeep Grand Cherokee in a private sale for a really great price."

"The Grand Cherokee is a nice vehicle and has lots of bells and whistles," Steve said.

"The thing is, Steve, as I said, I don't know anything about cars and I'm nervous about buying one privately without knowing if it was serviced properly. And that's where the favour I need comes in," Emma said. "I think the Grand Cherokee I'm considering was originally bought new here by the people selling it, Mary and Ethan Holdaway?"

"You can't be too careful when you're buying a used car not through a dealer, that's for sure. You don't know what you're getting," Steve said. "But it turns out that I know Mr. Holdaway. He's a regular customer. Buys all of his vehicles from us and gets them serviced here. I didn't know he still had the '23 Cherokee, haven't seen it in here for a while."

Emma leaned over the counter as far as she could so she was close to Steve and she watched him glance down at her breasts.

"Steve, could you just take a quick look at the service records for the Cherokee? Maybe the last time it was in? You know, so I know it was properly maintained before I buy it?" Emma asked.

"I don't know about giving out information from someone else's file," Steve said.

"How confidential can a vehicle maintenance file be?" Emma said with a smile as she remained as close as possible to Steve's face with the counter between them. "I'll owe you a coffee or maybe a drink when you get off work if you like."

"That drink sounds like a great idea," Steve said as he grabbed another quick look at Emma's breasts. "Okay, what the hell, let's have a look."

Emma leaned back from the counter as Steve went to the computer and started typing on the keyboard.

"Here it is, a 2023 Grand Cherokee, still listed under Mr. Holdaway's name in our service files," Steve said as he looked at the monitor.

"The last time it was in here was well over a year ago, but we didn't do any servicing on it. It went into our car wash for a full detailing service. Before that, there are dates going back to when it was bought, all for just routine maintenance, oil, lube and filter."

"That's great news, Steve!" Emma said enthusiastically and then asked, "What was the date the detailing was done?"

"Um, let's see," Steve said as he studied the monitor. "It was May 19th, 2023, at 3 pm."

"Thanks, Steve, you're a sweetheart," Emma said and then turned and started walking for the door.

"So, we going for that drink later today?" Steve called out to Emma's back as other waiting customers looked on.

"I'll call you, Steve," Emma said as she continued out the door.

Back sitting in her SUV, Emma took a deep breath and felt some guilt for taking advantage of an obviously nice guy. She took her phone out of her purse and pushed the speed dial for Shane's number. Looks like Shane's on the right path, she thought. Holdaway had his wife's car detailed on the same day that Paige Madison was murdered. A car he no longer has and didn't trade in with his usual dealer.

Chapter Twenty Eight - Present

Ethan Holdaway's home was a long, brick ranch-style house with a two-car attached garage on a wide, deep lot along a tree-lined street in an older section of Brantford's northwest.

Shane parked the Charger on the street in front of the house and noted the new, expensive Chrysler 300C sitting in the driveway. He assumed Ethan's wife Mary's vehicle was in the garage.

It was early Saturday morning, so Shane knew it was a safe bet that Holdaway would be home, which is where he wanted to talk to Ethan, catch him off guard here rather than the safe confines of the businessman's office.

Shane walked to the front door, pushed the bell, took a step back, and waited. A few moments went by and he was about to ring the bell again when Holdaway opened the door. He was wearing a light gray sweatsuit, his thinning hair hadn't been brushed yet and he didn't have on the glasses he normally wore.

"Mr. Holdaway, my name is Shane Daniels, I work with the lawyer Jason Burke," Shane said pleasantly.

"I know who you are," Holdaway answered flatly. "Why are you at my house? What do you want?" he asked in a very unfriendly tone.

"I want to talk to you about your relationship with Paige Madison," Shane answered.

"Paige Madison? Paige has been dead for a year and a half and as you know, she was murdered by my late business partner," Holdaway said.

"But some things have come to light about Paige's murder that I need to ask you about," Shane said.

"What kind of things!?" Holdaway asked, his irritation growing. "As everyone already knows, and I told the police, and I testified to at the trial, I barely knew Paige."

"But it turns out that's not true, is it Mr. Holdaway? That's why we need to talk," Shane said, keeping his voice even.

"I have nothing to say to you and I will not allow you into my home to spew some wild allegations," Holdaway said angrily. "If you have questions, you can talk to my lawyer, Vernon Styles. I'm sure you can find his contact info online," Holdaway said and started to close the door.

"Actually, Mr. Holdaway, I think it should be you calling Mr. Styles. In fact, you should do it right away and ask him to meet you at the Brantford Police Station in, I don't know, maybe a couple of hours," Shane said.

Holdaway stopped closing the door and said, "Why the hell should I do that?"

"Because if you don't talk to me right now, my next stop will be the Brantford Police where I will lay out everything I know and everything I suspect about you and Paige," Shane said. "I have no doubt that when I'm done, the police will have a lot of questions and you'll suffer the indignity of officers coming to your house and putting you in the back of a cruiser."

Holdaway stood holding the door half closed and stared at Shane, who stared right back and waited calmly for Holdaway to decide what he was going to do.

"Okay, come in and tell me what you think you know so I can tell you you're wrong and then get on with my weekend," Holdaway finally said as he opened the door fully and stepped aside to let Shane into the house.

"Who is it, dear?" Shane heard a woman ask from another room and he suspected it was the kitchen.

"It's just some last minute business stuff, Mary," Holdaway called out.

"Would you and your guest like some coffee?" Mary, who was still out of sight, said.

"No, we're fine. He won't be here long," Holdaway answered and then held out his left arm to indicate to Shane they would sit in the living room adjacent to the entryway. Shane chose to sit in a leather armchair while Holdaway sat on a matching sofa so they were facing each other.

"Okay, what is it that you think is so important that you have to bother me at my home?" Holdaway asked, his voice shaky with indignation.

"You murdered Paige Madison and coldly let your long time friend and business partner take the blame for it," Shane said and then added, "And your innocent friend, Gavin Benson, unable to face life in jail, killed himself."

"What are you talking about?" Holdaway asked. "Gavin killed Paige, was found guilty by a jury, and killed himself out of guilt."

"No, you killed Paige and I can prove it," Shane said.

"Really? How?" Holdaway asked and to Shane this apparently remorseless man sitting across from him was starting to sound smug. "Paige liked to take advantage of older men with some financial means who she knew had an eye for young, beautiful girls," Shane said, "And you fit the bill."

Holdaway leaned forward on the sofa to protest, but before he could say anything, Shane jumped in. "Forget your bullshit denials, Mr. Holdaway, and just listen," He said forcefully.

Shane then said that he first started to wonder about Holdaway's relationship with Paige because of something he read in the Benson trial transcript when he was being held captive by Josh Benson. Holdaway said he had seen the news coverage of Shane's abduction and was sorry it happened and couldn't believe the Josh he knew would do such a thing.

"During your testimony at the trial, you called Paige a flirt and when asked if she flirted with you, your answer was no because she knew better than to try that with you," Shane said. "I just couldn't get that exchange out of my head. She flirted with all the other men but not you? Was it because she didn't need to since you were already in a relationship? You said you had nothing to do with Paige, she was under Gavin's supervision and you really didn't know her. And yet you seemed to know enough about her to know she wouldn't try and flirt with you."

"That's it?" Holdaway responded. "Because Paige didn't flirt with me you think I killed her? Really?"

"Oh, that was just the seed," Shane said. "Actually, it was like an earworm, you know like a song you can't get out of your head. I couldn't let go of it and I didn't know why until I escaped from Josh Benson's basement room, got my head clear, started doing some digging and then everything fell into place."

While Holdaway just stared at him, Shane sat forward on his chair and continued, "Paige was living way beyond her means; a high rent apartment, a new car, nice clothes. We missed this fact, a critical error on our part, but the Crown didn't and subpoenaed the company's and Gavin's personal financial records. They didn't find any payments to Paige to help their case, just proof the business was in trouble."

"But over the past two days, with some help from a forensic accountant, I found Paige's benefactor," Shane said. "You handled the company's finances and with your partner Gavin's agreement, had set up an investment portfolio to grow a portion of the business's profits. The account contained mutual funds, a stock portfolio and real estate investments. There were a lot of complicated transactions between the three, all designed to mask the fact that some profits from the mutual funds and stocks were being diverted into the real estate account and paid out to CanCon Holdings, which happens to own the building where Paige was living."

"So what?" Holdaway said. "I was investing in lots of property around the city. It was just a coincidence."

"No, it wasn't," Shane responded. "I spoke to the Property Manager at Paige's building, Pete Vandenburg, and although it took some arm-twisting, well maybe more like threats if I was honest about it, he admitted that five thousand dollars came into an account once a month for Paige's rent. That's twice what was needed for the rent, but Mr. Vandenburg said Paige had access to withdraw money from the account. That money came from you."

"I'm finished listening to this bullshit from you!" Holdaway said angrily as he stood up. "I want you to leave now or I will call my lawyer and have him sue you for everything you own!"

"You and I both know you're not going to do that, Mr. Holdaway, so sit down," Shane said firmly. "I haven't told you about your wife's Jeep yet."

"What about my old Jeep?" Mary Holdaway asked as she entered the room carrying a tray with a carafe of coffee and two mugs. "I know you said no to coffee, Ethan, but I brought some anyway in case you changed your mind," she said.

"How long ago did you trade in your Jeep Grand Cherokee, Mrs. Holdaway?" Shane asked pleasantly while Ethan glowered at him.

"I'm not sure. It was well over a year ago," Mary said as she stood holding the tray. "I liked that Jeep but Ethan insisted I needed a new car."

"Just out of curiosity because I'm thinking of buying a new car, did you get your current vehicle here in town?" Shane asked Mary.

"We normally deal locally, but Ethan decided we would get a better price at a dealer in Hamilton," Mary replied with a smile.

"Okay, Mary, that's enough, this conversation doesn't concern you," Holdaway snapped at his wife. "Go back to the kitchen and take that goddam coffee with you."

Mary didn't react, she simply turned and walked out of the room.

"So, about the Jeep," Shane said. "On the day of Paige's murder, you left the office and didn't want the receptionist to put anything on her calendar about where you were going. I talked to Edna, a lovely and very conscientious woman, who said you told her you had to take Mary's Jeep to the dealer for repairs. But it didn't need to be fixed. You had it detailed."

"I really don't remember any of that," Holdaway said sharply.

"Yes you do," Shane said. "I'm going to track that Jeep down and even if you detailed it several times, if Paige was in that vehicle, forensic experts will find proof. They can find trace evidence at the microscopic level."

"That's enough!" Holdaway exclaimed as he stood up again. "Nothing you're claiming proves anything. I insist that you leave!"

Shane stood up but didn't make a move to leave and instead kept talking. "So here's what I think happened," he began, "As soon as Paige started working at Grand River Associates, she pegged you as an easy target for her charms. Before long, you're having sex and Paige talks you into setting her up in a nice apartment and taking care of her expensive tastes. Or maybe Paige insisted you look after her or she would talk to your wife. Then you find out Paige is sleeping with Gavin, your friend and partner, who says he and Paige are in love. You're furious because she's moved on to someone else and you're still paying for her nice lifestyle."

"So you go to her apartment," Shane continued, "Maybe there's an argument or maybe there's not, either way, you choke her to death and in your blind anger, you sexually mutilate her body. Paige lives on the ground floor so it's easier to make sure no one is around. You put her body in your wife's Jeep, drive to a field off Powerline Road and dump her body there like a piece of trash which, in your rage, you thought she was."

Holdaway didn't say a word or move from where he was standing. His face gave away nothing, but Shane could see the anger in his eyes.

"So how did I do? Was I close?" Shane asked.

Holdaway pointed at the front door and yelled, "Get out! You can't prove anything and I'm going to sue you for slander. Get the hell out!"

Shane turned and walked toward the front door and on the way, he glanced down the hallway to the kitchen and saw Mary Holdaway standing frozen in place in the doorway, still holding the tray with the coffee carafe and mugs. The shock of what she likely overheard had her eyes wide open, her mouth agape and tears running down her face.

"I'm sorry, Mrs. Holdaway," Shane muttered and then turned to her husband and said, "I lied about the police. They are, in fact, on their way to arrest you. They let me come and talk to you first as a courtesy because I found Paige's real killer and fixed a miscarriage of justice. Plus, I wanted the satisfaction of looking you in the face and calling you a cold-blooded killer."

Chapter Twenty Nine - A Week Later

Shane was sitting on a well-worn chair in a family waiting room located inside the Palliative Care Unit at the Brantford General Hospital, reading an online story on his phone's news feed and feeling pretty good about it.

The story detailed how Ethan Holdaway had finally been formally charged with second-degree murder in the death of Paige Madison and was in custody. Although getting bail is rare for anyone charged with murder, Holdaway's lawyer had argued successfully to have the businessman released on a surety and an ankle monitor, based on his lack of any criminal record.

Shane was a bit surprised to read that the Crown had seriously considered charging Holdaway with first-degree murder instead of second-degree, the charge Gavin Benson was wrongfully convicted of. But in the online story, prosecutor Even Gregory was quoted as saying that they believed Holdaway had intended to kill Paige before he left his office the day of the murder, so her death was clearly planned and deliberate.

It took the better part of a week to firm up the evidence against Holdaway that Shane had provided police. Mary Holdaway's Jeep Grand Cherokee was tracked to a resident of Caledonia, a town not far from Hamilton, and its owner was not too pleased when it was seized, put on the back of a flatbed truck, and taken to Ontario's top vehicle forensics facility in Toronto. In the area where the back of the passenger seat met the floor of the storage area, investigators found several hairs with roots still attached and in the crevice where the storage area floor butted up against the bottom of the back hatch door, they found traces of blood. DNA from both the hair and the blood were matched to Paige Madison.

Forensic experts also did another extensive search of Paige's former high-end apartment, a much more complicated task given that a young couple had been living there since Paige's death more than a year and a half ago. They collected dozens of prints and hairs, but even after eliminating evidence left by the new tenants, any prints found were either partial or too degraded. Too much time had passed.

But while Crown Prosecutor Evan Gregory went through the motions of having the apartment searched again, he felt he already had what he needed. At the time of Paige's murder, her apartment was searched and like this latest one, dozens of prints were found and most were identified as coming from Paige, Paige's parents, Ariel Durst and, eventually, Gavin Benson, once he was arrested and fingerprinted. There were other prints lifted in the apartment that were not in the system at that time, but are now because they belong to newly fingerprinted Ethan Holdaway. Gregory expected there would be a court challenge from Holdaway's lawyer over the admissibility of the prints, but he was confident it would not be successful.

A police forensic accountant confirmed what Shane had found regarding the connection between the business investment account handled exclusively by Holdaway and payments made to the management company of the building where Paige lived, as well as the fact that Paige had personal access to the money.

Holdaway pleaded not guilty during his first appearance in court, but Jason Burke had told Shane there have been several discussions since then between Holdaway's lawyer, Vernon Styles, and Gregory. Holdaway, through his lawyer, was apparently willing to admit that he had an affair with Paige and had been in her apartment a number of times. He was also willing to admit that he paid Paige's rent and gave her money, at first to keep her happy and then to keep her quiet. But Holdaway insists he did not kill Paige and his lawyer says they'll argue the killer had already been identified and found guilty by a jury.

Jason also told Shane he had heard around the courthouse that Styles was preparing a diminished capacity defence and would argue that Holdaway was suffering from a mental breakdown, and severe emotional distress, when he killed Paige and dumped her body, and was therefore not responsible for his actions. In Canada, the defence of diminished responsibility reduces a murder conviction to one of manslaughter.

Shane had just completed reading the Holdaway article on his phone and was going through his emails when he looked up and saw Melissa Edwards, Gavin Benson's daughter, enter the family waiting room and smile at him.

Shane put his phone in his pocket and stood, but Melissa put her hand up and pointed to the empty chair beside him, so he sat back down and she joined him. Melissa looked like a younger version of her mother, Alison, with fine features, thin lips, green eyes and wavy auburn hair.

"How's he doing?" Shane asked, referring to Melissa's brother Josh, who was in a room just up the hall from where they were sitting.

"They've put him on a ventilator and are pumping drugs into him in case he's in pain, which they don't know for sure because he's no longer able to communicate," Melissa said softly. "His eyes are open all the time and he looks at you if you speak to him, but the doctors don't know if he's lucid enough to understand what you're saying. I tried to see if he would blink for yes or no, but he just kept staring at me."

Some tears had formed in Melissa's eyes and were now slowly making their way down her cheeks. She reached into the purse on her lap and took out a tissue to wipe them away.

"Do they know how long he might have?" Shane asked in a quiet voice.

"It could be anytime," Melissa answered. "Since he was arrested, the tumour in his brain has grown at an alarming rate and is slowly shutting down all of his motor functions. He can no longer breathe on his own."

"And you don't mind if I have a short visit with him?" Shane asked.

"Of course not," Melissa said. "We're so grateful that you cleared my father's name and are still in shock that Ethan killed Paige and let Dad take the blame. I loved my dad and didn't want to believe the things that were said about him during his trial. I know my mom will never forgive him for his affair with Paige, but I know she still loved him."

Melissa turned in her chair, put her hands over Shane's and said, "I'm so sorry about what Josh did to you. He adored his father, but I had no idea that he would go to such lengths to prove his innocence."

"The brain tumour clouded his reasoning. I've managed to forgive him for what he did," Shane said.

"I hope you don't suffer any lingering effects from what Josh put you through," Melissa said.

Shane didn't answer and instead stood up and said, "I'll go see Josh now. Good luck to you and your family."

"I'm just sad that my father and my brother won't see my daughter grow up," Melissa said as tears continued to run down her face.

Shane left the waiting room, turned left, and walked down the hall to Josh's room where he saw a Corrections Officer sitting on a chair beside the door. Although he was in end-of-life care, Josh was still technically a prisoner and therefore had to remain under guard.

Shane nodded to the officer and entered the room where there was a single bed. Josh was covered to his chest by a blanket with his arms on top, an IV on his left hand leading to a pole with several clear bags. A clip on his pointer finger carried wires to a series of monitors and the room was filled with the constant sound of the ventilator pumping air into Josh's lungs.

There was a chair beside the bed, but Shane didn't sit. Josh's eyes, which were staring at the ceiling, turned and looked at Shane, but Shane didn't see any acknowledgment in them.

"I'm sorry for what has happened to you, Josh," Shane said. "But I want you to know that you were right in believing in your father's innocence. I just wish you had gone about trying to prove it in a different way, but I don't blame you for what you did. I sincerely regret that your father took his own life before Jason and I had a chance to clear his name. But thanks to you, he died an innocent man."

Shane looked down momentarily at the former soldier who continued to stare at him and was about to leave when he saw Josh reach out with his right hand and weakly squeeze Shane's wrist. It only lasted a second and there was no change in the blank expression on Josh's face. Shane nodded at him and walked out of the room.

Later that day when Shane got home, he ordered a pizza and sat with Emma and Lan at the kitchen table working their way through the two boxes; one just cheese and pepperoni because that was all Lan liked and one fully loaded except for pineapple, which Shane refused to eat, insisting that fruit didn't belong on pizza.

While they were eating, Emma kept sneaking glances at Shane, to see if she could tell by his face how he was feeling, even though he said he was fine when he arrived home. He had been through a lot and Emma knew it had taken a toll as signaled last night when Shane suddenly sat up in bed, covered in sweat.

"I'm okay, just a nightmare," he had said to Emma when she sat up to check on him. Emma was glad that Shane had agreed to a few sessions with her psychiatrist friend Charlene Anderson.

"How's Jason doing?" Emma asked as she reached over for another slice of pizza.

"Like me, he's still beating himself up over what we missed in the Benson case and he's been in a rather bad mood because of it," Shane answered.

Jason tried to take full responsibility for the mistakes that were made that led to Gavin Benson's murder conviction, but Shane would have no part of it, saying he should have taken a much closer look at Paige, talked to more people about her, and not just accept the word of people like her friend Ariel Durst who said Paige was a sweet, innocent girl who just happened to like older men. And worst of all, he should have noticed well before the trial started that Paige was living beyond her means.

Jason was the most upset at what he called his failure to read the jury during the trial and claimed he was losing his touch. He was convinced he had demonstrated to the jurors that the Crown had not proven Benson's guilt beyond a reasonable doubt, but he was dead wrong. Shane tried to tell him that no one could have predicted that every member of the jury appeared to have decided right from the start, no matter what they heard, that Gavin Benson was a liar and a cheat.

When they were close to finishing their pizza, Shane suggested they take a couple of days off and drive up north to show Lan Paisley and Port Elgin since they'd been so busy over the past year and hadn't had an opportunity to take her to visit Shane's hometown and the tourist town where he went to high school.

"Will we be going to Uncle Ben's restaurant?" Lan asked.

"Uncle Ben?" Emma wondered out loud. "Did Ben ask you to call him that?"

"No, I just thought it would be a nice thing to do," Lan said and then asked Shane, "Are you sure I won't get sick eating the food at Uncle Ben's restaurant like he says I will?"

"I'm absolutely sure!" Shane replied. "Ben always says that about his food, but he's joking."

"I really like Uncle Ben," Lan said. "He tries hard not to swear in front of me, but he can't do it, and he makes me laugh."

"Yeah, he's a real comedian," Emma said sarcastically.

Lan giggled and it made Shane feel the best he had in weeks.

Murray Moffatt